# Centurion

## Mark's Gospel as a Thriller

## Book One

Ryan Casey Waller

ISBN-13: 9780615902982
ISBN-10: 0615902987
Library of Congress Control Number: 2013918898
Interlochen Ink, Dallas, TX

*To the students of All Saints' Episcopal School—especially the Class of 2014—*
*this one's for y'all.*

# CHAPTER 1

*North America, 2099 AD*

I took the money.

I remember it like it was yesterday. My father had called it a war chest, said it was the weapon of my future—my education. I knew this money was all he and my mother had. How could I take it?

But my mother had insisted. "What do you want us to do with it?" she said. "You're the reason we saved this money all these years. If you refuse, our lives will be wasted."

I can still see myself sitting on that old creaking train, scared out of my mind. I knew good and well that when a young man left the South, he never came back.

As the train groaned beneath the weight of its battered steel and gathered speed, I looked out the window and saw my father nod farewell. My mother couldn't let go of me so stoically. She ran alongside the train with tears streaming from her blue eyes until she collided into the iron chest of an ungodly tall centurion. When I close my eyes, I still see his blond hair whipping out from beneath his golden helmet. Just before we disappeared into the King Charles Tunnel, I saw him grab my mother and drag her back to where my father had been standing. My father was already gone.

That was three years ago.

Today I'm coming home, but I haven't done what my parents sent me out West to do. I haven't finished school and never will. My parents won't be waiting for me on the landing where we said our good-byes. They're gone now, and I won't see them again.

The train jerks as its brakes screech against the hot rolled steel of the rails. The behemoth slows and breathes thick waves of billowing smoke before coming to a stop inside the once magnificent station of the South. With its thirty-foot ceilings, ornate murals, and crystal chandeliers, this station was once the pride of a community. Now it's nothing but a thin, pathetic shell of its former self. The murals haven't been cleaned in decades, and most of the chandeliers were shattered during the Great War. Those that survived hang unlit. The station looks like the rest of the South and the people who live here—exhausted.

The slim door of my cabin opens, and the conductor appears. He's short, with a potbelly and a handlebar mustache. He examines the passengers' papers in a gruff yet efficient manner. Behind him follows a centurion who eyes each passenger with a mixture of suspicion and hatred. He's large, like the man who grabbed my mother, but not nearly as tall. I have the contours of that man's body memorized and will know him when I see him.

There are only seven passengers in my cabin. Leaving the West to travel south isn't a smart thing to do. The growing unrest and coming war has made my home a dangerous place. The man across the aisle shakes as he scrambles to produce his papers. *Nervous.*

My papers are resting on my lap, where they've been for the final hour of the journey. This is the moment I've been waiting for, and I'm ready. One more test and I'll be home.

The lies already have been told.

More important, the lies have been believed. All I have to do is keep from retching onto my boots, which I'm on the verge of doing. *My turn.*

"Papers," the conductor barks. Not a question, an order.

I hold up my ID card and travel visa for him and the centurion to see. The conductor snatches them from my hand while the centurion glares down at me from behind the dark shield of his helmet. I stare resolutely at my reflection in his shield. I'm beginning to look older. At twenty-three I'm no longer the fat-faced boy who left this place. My visage is longer, my blue eyes a shade darker, and my sinewy muscles hardened from countless hours of running sand dunes, flipping oversize tires, and learning to kill. I departed this place a boy; I return a man.

The conductor examines my ID card and says, "American?"

Keeping my eyes fixed on the centurion, I reply, "That's what it says on the card." I've vowed not to be intimidated by these soldiers.

The conductor furrows his brow. "Yes, young man, I'm able to read. I'm not some ignorant Southerner. But I'm asking you a question, a privilege that won't be afforded a third time. Are you an American?"

I look the conductor in the eye. "Yes, born and raised here in the ignorant South."

"And your reason for leaving the West? Your visa says you're still a student." He checks his watch. "If I'm not mistaken, the fall semester starts in less than a month."

Here comes the hard part. My eyes nervously bounce from the conductor to the centurion, who has lifted his shield to examine me closer. His face is classic Nordic: bright blue eyes, snowy white skin, and a sharp nose that curves down like the beak of a bird. But his expression is anything but centurion. This man's face isn't full of hatred. Instead he looks at me as if admiring a work of art. This isn't what I want.

My eyes dart back to the conductor. "My parents were abducted by the Kingdom," I say. "I've come home to handle their affairs. The Office of Record has already processed their papers, and they're waiting for me at their house."

The conductor opens my travel visa, a tiny blue booklet with a golden etched profile of King Charles's face. "Deacon Larsen. It says here that your father is a laborer and your mother a maid. Their assets can't be too extensive. And you mean 'selected' not 'abducted,' don't you?"

"My father was a laborer, sir. And my mother was a maid. And..." *Easy,* I tell myself. I clear my throat and say, "Yes, sir. I'm sorry. They were *selected* by the Kingdom to serve in the northern camps...where they both died, unfortunately."

The conductor yawns. "They died honorably in service to the Holy King Charles. All honor be given to his name."

"All honor be given to his name," the centurion and I repeat in submissive, robotic unison.

Bile rises from my stomach and climbs the walls of my throat.

The conductor acts as if nothing has happened. "You're an only child?" he says.

3

I swallow my vomit and feel it torch my esophagus on the downward plunge. "Yes," I say through clenched teeth.

"How long do you expect to stay?"

"I've been granted a year's leave from my studies."

He lifts an eyebrow. "A long time to suspend an education."

"I've applied to take courses at the University of the South."

The conductor grins. "Bit of a joke, right? Compared to the education you're receiving out West in Old California? Do they even teach medicine in this backcountry of slaves and misfits?"

"They offer courses on anatomy and chemistry."

The conductor grunts. "You're to report to the Office of Record every Monday at noon to check in with your supervisor. Since today is Sunday, you have tomorrow's itinerary. Understood, young medicine man?"

I nod. The centurion's ruddy face shines with interest, as if he's on the verge of asking a burning question. But of course he doesn't. Centurions rarely speak to Americans, unless it's to bark an order or inform someone they're about to be shot.

"Very well then." The conductor flips shut my visa and hands it and my ID card back to me. "Go in peace to serve the Kingdom and the venerable King Charles."

"May the gods ever help me," I say, feeling the bile return.

The conductor and the centurion move past me and out the back door of the cabin.

And there it is. *I made it home!*

The official story is that I'm returning to the South to handle the affairs of my deceased parents. But it's a lie. My parents are dead, and no amount of pomp and ceremony will bring them back from the grave. The real reason I abandoned the safety of my studies—studies that would have given me a privileged life in medicine—is that I've decided to betray the Kingdom.

I haven't come home to handle petty paperwork. I've come home to avenge my parents' deaths and join the resistance. I have no interest in blessing the dead; I've come to bury more.

# CHAPTER 2

The Southern heat wraps me in an unwanted embrace of moisture and defeat as I step from the train. Three years living by the sea has made me soft to the climate, and I've forgotten how oppressive the summer air can be. I wipe sweat off my face with my sleeve and move cautiously from the train into the station. I'm fully aware that I now walk among people who will kill me should my motives be uncovered.

I watch as families embrace with the joy created by long, uncertain absences. Mothers welcome sons with wide-open arms. Husbands kiss wives with abandon, as if their children aren't watching. Fathers lift smiling children high into the air; their laughter colors the air with bliss.

But none of this brings me joy.

I collect my trunk and drag it outside the station to wait for a taxi.

There I discover the rumors are true; the Kingdom's presence is everywhere. Lining the streets are banners with large images of King Charles's face printed on them. The king is scandalously young; he looks like a teenager. He has tousled brown hair and bright-green eyes. The muscles in his face are taut, as if he's ready to shout an unholy order. *Ruthless* is the word that flashes through my brain.

No one in the taxi line speaks.

As I wait, my mind wanders through the tumultuous history of recent years. Travel privileges were revoked only two months after I left for Old California. The era of Great Uncertainty finally had come to an end when the English squashed the Chinese uprising and seized governmental power in this country once and for all. It had been a full decade since any single authority had ruled the vast land that was once the USA.

When I left there were maybe five thousand centurions in the South. The giant Nordic who took my mother represented the threat of what was to come. I'm told there are now more than one hundred thousand centurions infecting our land. If this is true, King Charles understands what's happening—that this is where the rebellion will start

This means the centurions, who are coldblooded killers, must be dealt with accordingly. When it was certain the English would take over, the Brits sent an open call to the world's mercenaries—"Come! Fight! Get rich!" That's all it took. Hundreds of ships steamed into Old New York Harbor and dumped countless soldiers onto once mighty shores.

The Kingdom organized these killers into what is now called the "Centurion Guard" and charged them with squashing any uprising that opposed King Charles's control of the country. And that's precisely what they did.

My taxi pulls up. The driver is a black man who introduces himself as "Miles." "You don't look like you're from around here," he says. We pull onto a skinny street jammed with traffic. Miles rolls down his window. Car horns blare, and the smell of burning rubber wafts into the cab. My sweaty back sticks to the cheap vinyl of the seat.

"Born and raised," I say.

"No accent?"

"Never had one."

"What brings you home?"

Our eyes meet mine in the rearview. *What brings you home?* I've heard rumors about secret phrases used to test a person to see whose side he or she is on. I can't be sure if this is such a query, but it feels that way. I open my mouth then shut it.

Finally I say, "My parents died. I'm here to manage their affairs."

"I'm sorry," Miles says warmly. "You're young."

We lumber through heavy traffic, and I stare out the window. This city, Oxford, as it is newly named, has become an odd blend of industry and desolation. Although it was once a budding metropolis, the Great War reduced its vitality to life support. As we near downtown, I see an old high-rise that once projected two-hundred-foot-tall holograms across its glass. You could see the blazing images from anywhere in the city. The building is now draped in what must be the largest and most grotesque banner in the world; King Charles's face covers the entire thing. It's a two-hundred-foot-tall idol. The rest of the skyline is a patchwork; some buildings are lit, others dark and abandoned.

Miles snakes his way through downtown traffic before jetting off onto side streets.

"You're a Southerner?" I say.

He keeps his eyes on the road. "Yes, but I left for many years and have just recently returned."

"What brought you back?"

His eyes appear in the mirror. "A job."

I motion to the crumbling taxicab. "This one?"

He shakes his head. "No. I came home for a…project—something I could do only in Oxford. Still sounds strange calling it that…*Oxford.*"

Miles turns onto my street and parks in front of the house where I grew up. It's nothing more than a fat cube of adobe with a tattered roof and a red door. I regard it briefly then look away. "I hear many Southerners are coming home," I say, "which seems odd, given the scarcity of work to be had."

"Not to mention the violence," Miles says. "This city is on the verge of chaos, my friend."

"So I hear."

Miles twists in his seat and extends an outstretched palm. I lean forward and shake his hand. He says, "So tell me then, my friend, why *have* you come home?"

He squeezes my hand hard, and I feel as though my chest might burst open. He's begging me to say it, and it's driving me mad. I need someone with whom I can share my anger and my unquenchable thirst for revenge. I desperately want to tell him the truth, to confess everything. I decide to do it.

But then he releases his grip.

"I told you," I say, my voice thick with anxiety, "I've come to bury the memory of my parents."

Miles holds my stare for a long second before returning his gaze to the front of the car. "My teacher says we ought to let the dead bury the dead."

"I don't know what that means," I mutter, peeling some worn bills from my wallet and handing them up front.

Miles sighs. "I know you don't."

I swing the door wide and climb out of the cab. Miles helps me lift my trunk and sets it on the sidewalk. Then he slinks back into his tired yellow cab. This man is either sincerely crestfallen that I haven't confessed my true motives or a very fine actor. He puts the car in drive and begins to pull away.

I call after him, "Miles!" I trot across the few yards that separate us. "What's the project, the one you could only do in Oxford? I...might be interested in hearing more about it."

A smile breaks wide across his face, revealing a mouth of brilliantly glowing white teeth. He wags a long finger. "Yes, my friend! I suspected that might be the case." The smile vanishes as Miles cranes his neck to see if any cars are coming down the road. There's no one else in sight. "Meet me tomorrow night," he says, "after sunset, at the entrance to the park downtown. Are you familiar with it?"

"Of course."

"Tell no one."

I nod and swallow hard.

"Rest well, my friend," he says seriously. "You're going to need your strength in the days to come."

Then Miles is gone, and I'm left with nothing but the crippling thought that I've just tied a noose around my neck.

# CHAPTER 3

I thought coming home would be a comfort. If I couldn't have my parents, at least I could have their space, linger at their photographs. Perhaps catch a whiff of my mother's vanilla-and-tobacco perfume on her pillowslip. Maybe use the crisp tonic of my father's aftershave. These were the small mercies I hoped God would grant me.

But this is torture, and the only scent the house emits is of mildew and dust. I spent three hours last night weeping uncontrollably, curled up in a fetal position. I wept until my body gave up on my soul. I tried to recite the prayers of my ancestors but quit before I could form the words. The traditions are supposed to be my guide through the valley of death, but I don't even have the strength to stand and follow.

Grieving alone is something no person should do. Solitary bereavement is a fate worse than death, which last night I considered the finer alternative to the coming sunrise.

*My dark thought.*

I spend the morning handling the paperwork I've allegedly come home to address. There isn't much. My parents owned this house outright and left it to me in their will, along with a few other possessions: petty cash stored at the Oxford Trust, my father's motorcycle, and a key to a safe-deposit box. The box, according to the papers, is being held for me at the Oxford Trust.

The key surprises me. What did my father own that needed to be kept in a safe-deposit box? Antiques and heirlooms are rare finds in the South. What the Great War didn't destroy was either stolen by anarchists or traded or sold for the essentials: food, gasoline, and money. But my family always has been poor, so we didn't have much from the start. I can't imagine what's in that box. I make plans to visit the trust after my appointment at the Office of Record.

I kill what's left of my morning drinking coffee and packing away photographs. If I'm to live in this house, I need it devoid of sentiment. I can't bear the sight of my mother's blue eyes or my father's broad shoulders. The time for mourning is over.

Besides…I'll see my parents soon enough.

The Office of Record is located in a redbrick, two-story building on the edge of downtown. I leave an hour early and make a slow walk of it. The rumors are true. A centurion is perched on nearly every block. Each warrior is dressed in red body armor and a golden helmet and carries an assault rifle.

For Southerners guns are strictly forbidden. Punishment for possession is immediate execution—no jury and no trial. I behold more guns on this walk than I've seen in all my twenty-three years. I don't know how to feel about that, but something inside me stirs. The hairs on my neck bristle.

At the Office of Record, I receive a number and am told to wait in a room with ten other Americans who've clearly seen better days. The gentleman next to me smells of oil and his boots are tattered and ancient looking. A woman my mother's age stares at me and I know what she's thinking. *My son was your age when they took him.* The waiting room is sterile, brightly lit, and far too cold. Unlike in Miles's dilapidated taxicab, the air conditioning in this building is in good working order.

No one speaks; everyone seems nervous. As Americans, we limit our contact with Kingdom authorities. We're a people not to be trusted, and the Kingdom looks for any and every reason to "select" us for work in the camps. Just coming to the Office of Record is a fantastic way to kick-start that process.

Twenty minutes later a stunning woman is ushered from the office, where I'll soon be summoned. She's young and has long, disheveled black hair. She's crying and wiping tears away as she walks, fumbling with her papers. I should avert my eyes and mind my own business. This isn't the place to stick your nose in other people's affairs.

And I would do that, if she weren't so terribly gorgeous.

But she is.

Her eyes sparkle, and I'm positive I've never seen eyes so dark; they're black as the night. Her skin is a cocoa brown and looks to be as smooth as silk.

*She's from Mexico,* I think.

I know from my history courses that millions of Mexicans used to live in this region, but now they're as rare as falling stars. I've never actually spoken to a Mexican, as they're forbidden to live in the West.

The woman glances my way for a moment before ducking her face into her tiny hands. When she passes me, she looks up once more, and our eyes slam into one another. Her stare is electric.

I've never been in love. But if this dark-eyed young woman were to speak to me, I believe that would change. She's magnificent, and my body immediately aches for her.

A moment later she's gone, but her scent lingers—the delicate smell of woman that I've known only from a distance, lavender and peach. I have an irrational urge to bolt from my seat and chase after her, to grab her by the arm and ask why she's crying, to see if there's anything I can do to help. But before I can make any stupid decisions, a woman calls my name.

It's my turn.

I let go of the exotic woman and stand to face the Kingdom and the authority of King Charles. This will be my toughest test to try to go unnoticed. If I'm unable to convince these people of my motives, my mission will end before it's begun.

My supervisor is a petite woman named Dr. Stone—no first name, just Dr. Stone. She's in her midfifties, with short blond hair, a small button of a nose, and oversize blue eyes. She's surprisingly attractive for a Kingdom bureaucrat. She smiles warmly when I enter her office and motions for me to sit in a leather chair across from her powerful-looking desk. It's a desk that screams authority.

"Good afternoon, Mr. Larsen," she says tenderly as I sit. "May I call you 'Deacon'?"

Dr. Stone can call me anything she wants, as long as I get out of here without handcuffs around my wrists. I nod.

"Excellent," she says. Her voice is high and polished, as if she has attended a finishing school where they teach women to speak in properly aristocratic tones. She has the classic English accent of the elite. "My name is Dr. Stone. I'm your assigned supervisor."

"I was told to report here every Monday at noon," I say, wanting to dismiss with formalities.

Dr. Stone closes a large file on her desk. My name, Deacon Larsen, is printed in bold black letters on its cover.

"Yes," she replies. "That's quite right. It's vital that you not miss a single meeting with me. One absence and your travel privileges could be revoked. Permanently," she adds, elongating each syllable until the word becomes impossibly long. "Which means you wouldn't be able to travel back West to finish your schooling."

"That would be awful," I say, hearing how hallow and facetious my voice sounds compared to hers. Sweat gathers beneath my arms. These are nervous sweats that always accompany my lies. I desperately wish to be a convincing liar, but I don't have the genetic makeup for it. The truth sits like a weight on my tongue, begging to be dropped off on a set of ears.

As I sit here, trying to lie, my brain silently screams the truth. *I'm never traveling west. If I make it out of Oxford—and that's a major if—I'll head north, marching with an army straight toward the heart of the Kingdom. And that's where I'll die.*

Dr. Stone laughs. "Yes, I'm sure the prospect of living in dumpy old Oxford isn't all that appealing to an ambitious lad like yourself. The West has much more to offer." Dr. Stone leans back in her chair to signal our conversation will now be casual and friendly, just an old chat between two trusted friends. She smiles. "Your file says you wish to train as a physician. Is this accurate?"

"That's right."

"What sparked your interest in medicine?"

"I don't know."

"And you still plan to become a physician?"

I shrug. "Of course."

"You're not worried about taking a full year off from your studies? And how that might affect your chances of admission to medical school?"

"I'm pretty good at school," I mumble. "I'll be all right."

"Are you always this rude in the presence of authority? Or is it just women you detest?"

"No," I say, sitting up straight in my chair.

A dry grin spreads across Dr. Stone's face. "Do you have a girlfriend back on the coast? Some little tart you fancy?"

I shake my head.

"If you did," she says, "you probably wouldn't tell me, would you?"

"I'm sorry…I don't know what that has to do with my reporting here. Just tell me what I need to do, please."

Dr. Stone grins again, leans forward, and rests her elbows on her mahogany desk. Her grin vanishes. "You don't like me," she says. "I understand that. I'm English and you're American. On top of that, your parents perished in the camps. You probably hate every snotty English face you see. It wouldn't surprise me if you were imagining a scene in which I meet a violent death. Am I right? Hmm? Are you, young Deacon, wondering what it'd feel like to wrap your hands around my neck and squeeze the life out of my body? To squeeze my beautiful body until my limbs stop flailing and my chest heaves one last desperate time before my eyes roll to the back of my head?"

I start to speak, to stop this crazy woman from talking, but I feel like I've been kicked in the gut by the hoof of a horse. I inhale, but no air fills my lungs. My head pounds as if someone has taken a mallet to it. *How did she read me so fast? What have I done to give myself away?* Then it hits me. *Miles…the cab driver. He's a spy. I'll kill him.*

I shake my head furiously. "I don't know what you're talking about, ma'am." My voice sounds even cheaper than before, the words evaporating the second they leave my tongue. I can see it in her eyes; she knows I'm lying. "I would never—"

Dr. Stone holds up her hand for me to stop. I obey. She rises gracefully from her desk and pads around to the front, where she sits on top of the expensive wood and crosses her legs toward me. Our bodies are now inches from each other. The toe of her stiletto taps sharply against my shin. I swallow hard as her perfume crawls across my face.

"Why have you come home, Deacon?" she says, the tenderness in her voice returning. "The Office of Record made sure that your parents' home was well secured and that the appropriate documents were left inside for you.

Anything that needed to be done could have waited until the spring when you finished school. We make it a point to care for the families of those chosen for the camps, especially those who die honorably in service. Everyone in this town knew your parents. No one would have disturbed their home."

I clear my throat. "It felt wrong to be so far away. I needed to come here, to see it all for myself."

A sharp line extends across Dr. Stone's forehead. *"To see what?"*

"Nothing. I don't know…the house. I wanted to read the will with my own eyes; I needed closure."

Dr. Stone takes a long, hard, hungry look at me. She searches for truth, for authenticity, for what lies behind my eyes. I pray to God she's not good at reading people.

"What sort of doctor are you?" I say.

"A psychologist."

*Fantastic.*

"A doctor of the mind," I say.

"Common misunderstanding."

"What is?"

"Psychologists don't only study the mind; we study human behavior. We analyze *why* people do the things they do. You're a nice-looking young man."

"Thanks." I shift rigidly in my seat.

"You remind me of my own son. Your eyes are wonderfully blue." She looks me up and down, her eyes feasting on every inch of my body. "You're thick and strong. Why do you dress so formally?"

I take a self-conscious look at myself. It's true—I don't dress like a student; I dress like I'm already a doctor. My father taught me never to dress for the role I have in life but for the role I want to play. I wear slacks and a sport coat. Today my pants are gray and my jacket blue. My father said, "The face you wear tells the world how to treat you." I wear serious clothes and a serious face.

"Something my father taught me."

"I imagine you're quite the athlete."

"I'm all right."

She winks. "You're more than all right."

I don't know what to make of Dr. Stone. She simultaneously strikes me as an all-knowing supervisor and a psycho I should keep my eyes on at all times. Neither scenario bodes well for me. As my supervisor, she has absolute authority over me. If she wanted, she could have me sent back West immediately. And that would represent the mildest form of punishment she has at her discretion. Should she suspect my motives aren't precisely as I've stated in my travel visa, she could have me arrested and sent north to prison in less than a day's time. There's no such thing as due process in the South. Not for Americans. We're charged, convicted, and sentenced in a single day and by a single authority—even when the punishment is death.

I *need* Dr. Stone to like me. At the very least, I need her to believe me.

"I think we're getting off on the wrong foot," I say. "I didn't sleep much last night. I don't hate you, Doctor. And I don't hate the English. I may come from the South, but I've been a student in the West for three years. I understand what the English are doing, and I fully support it. In fact if I score well enough on my exams, I plan to do my residency in the north at Kingdom Hospital. I'm not some uneducated Southerner looking to raise hell. I want to be a model citizen for my fellow Americans, showing them how we ought to behave and properly submit to King Charles. I'm not here to cause any trouble."

Dr. Stone reveals nothing. *Maybe.* She sits quietly and glares at me. Then she raises her hand and beckons me closer with her index finger. I lean forward in my chair.

"Closer," she whispers, curling her finger like a witch enticing a child to the boiling stew. I slide to the edge of my chair until my legs are pressed firmly against hers. She leans down and puts her mouth next to my ear and whispers, "You're a bad liar, Deacon—outrageously bad. No man in his right mind leaves the life you had in the West to come here, to this miserable dump of a city— unless he's interested in picking a fight." She blows hotly into my ear. "Are interested in a fight, Deacon?"

I start to say something, to tell her she's lost her mind, but her hand clasps my throat with a supernatural strength, her fingernails digging into my skin and cutting off my air. She spits into my ear, "My eyes are on you. Should you so much as sneeze in a manner that perturbs my sensibilities, I'll have your head on my desk. I won't be sending you back to school. There's only one way out of Oxford for you, and that's north—to the bloody camps."

She releases her grip, and I fall out of my chair and onto the floor, gasping for air. Dr. Stone's face spins circles above me as the room grows dark, and only one thought races through my mind. *You're bloody well right.*

# CHAPTER 4

I vibrate with anger as I enter the Oxford Trust. It would be my luck that of all the possible supervisors in the Kingdom, I get the one who's certifiably insane. *Dr. Stone.* Just thinking of her name makes my blood boil. I laugh darkly at the irony of a crazy shrink holding the keys to my fate. Perfect.

*No, Doctor, I wasn't imagining your death—but I am now.*

My face is flushed as I approach the bank teller. I self-consciously pat at the scratch marks on my neck and discover I'm bleeding. I rub the blood between my fingers and try to smear it off. Dr. Stone gripped me with a ferocious power I wouldn't have thought she was capable of unleashing. She's so small. I shove my bloody, shaky hand into my pocket and introduce myself to the teller, whose nametag reads, "Jude."

"What can I do for you?" Jude says.

"I'm here to settle my parents' accounts," I say softly. I pull the paperwork from my pants pocket and hand it to Jude, a guy who looks about five years older than me. He's tall, with wide shoulders, flaming-red hair, and a gap between his two front teeth.

"Excellent," he says.

Jude takes the papers from the counter and examines them. He then punches a few keys on an outdated computer and waits while the old machine does its dilapidated thinking. I've heard rumors that the Office of Record and the banks are the only establishments in the South that still have computers. But it's hard to call the dinosaur Jude is working on an actual computer. The thing must be twenty years old. The relic finishes grinding, and when it does, his face flinches. He flickers his eyes away from the screen and onto me, then returns his gaze to the screen.

"You're Mr. Larsen?" he says. "Deacon…Larsen?"

"I am."

He moves the computer mouse with an unsteady hand. "Yes, OK then. Give me a moment. This won't take long."

"Is there a problem?"

Jude clicks the mouse once more before tearing a sheet of paper from a yellow legal pad. He scribbles something on it with a blue ink pen, takes a deep breath, and slides the paper under the bulletproof glass that separates us. I reach for the paper and pull it slowly toward me. Jude's note contains a single number.

"What's this?"

His face is expectant, like he's waiting to receive important but potentially disastrous news. "Your balance, sir."

Panic floods my voice like water into a sinking ship. "Of what? *Debt?* For the love of the one true God, please don't tell me my parents owed this amount to the bank."

Jude smiles and glances at the tellers on either side of him. Neither is paying any attention to us. In a soft voice, he says, "No. The account is in the black, sir. That number represents the cash your parents have deposited in our vault. Would you like to make a withdrawal?"

My mouth goes dry, and my tongue sticks to the roof of my mouth. My knees are weak, my arms buttery, my insides watery. "I...don't understand. You're saying this money belongs to my parents?"

Jude shakes his head. "No, sir. I'm not saying that at all. I'm saying this money belongs to *you.*"

I look once more at the messy handwriting and read the number slowly in my head.

*777,321.40.*

The sheer size of the figure hurts my brain. "But...this is a fortune. There must be some mistake. My parents weren't wealthy. They barely had enough money to pay for—"

"There has been no mistake," Jude says, interrupting me. "You can rest assured of that. Now I believe you're also in possession of a key to the safe-deposit box. Do you have it with you?"

*The key! I almost forgot.*

"Uh…yeah," I say, digging it from my pocket. "I have it right here."

Jude motions to his right. "If you'll give me a moment, I'll meet you by the red door and accompany you to the vault where your box is located."

I nod and Jude disappears. I snatch the sheet of paper with the monstrous number written on it and shove it deep inside my pocket, where it immediately morphs into a fifty-pound weight. On unsteady legs I shuffle toward the red door. Virtually no thoughts run through my mind as I try to come to grips with the fact that I've just won the lottery.

The paper burns hot and heavy against my leg as I wait.

The red door swings open, and I step from the lobby into a long hallway with brown shag carpet. It's deathly quiet. Jude silently leads me to the end of the hallway and through a secured steel door. We're now standing in a small room lined with safe-deposit boxes from floor to ceiling. The room is brightly lit, and there's no furniture, save for a small wooden table. A constant low hum makes the room feel as if it's buried deep underground.

I'm not afraid of small spaces, but if I were, I imagine this would be a distressing room, as it's roughly the size of an oversize elevator. The humming noise grows louder.

Jude presents me his hands, palms up, and asks for the key. I give it to him, and he retrieves another key from his pocket. "Both are needed to open the box," he clarifies. "But there's one last bit of information I'll need from you."

"What?"

"The password," he says, expectancy once again painted on his freckled face.

"I don't have a password. Just the key."

"The password," Jude says deliberately, "will be given by *you* after I've provided the stimulus."

"The what?" I say.

"The stimulus is a question written by your father. I'll repeat the question, verbatim, to you. Then you'll provide me with the password. If not, the box will remain locked."

"Where's the question?"

Jude points at his temple. "Right here."

"You have it memorized?"

He nods.

"OK," I say. "I'll try...but I can't guarantee I'll know the answer."

Jude grins tightly, and I see sweat beads on his forehead. The man clearly knows something I don't. "Are you ready?"

"I have no idea," I say.

"Don't answer until you're positive you know the correct response. You may only offer one reply. If it's incorrect, I'll immediately usher you out of this vault, and you won't receive another opportunity. These are your father's explicit instructions. So *please*, think carefully before you speak." Jude takes a deep breath. "For what purpose have you come home, my son? Speak openly, for I'm your father, and you're my son. There's nothing you can't tell me."

Jude nods when he's finished reciting the stimulus. It's my turn now.

Hearing the words of my father on a stranger's lips unnerves me, as if I'm hearing his voice from the grave. My emotion, however, is soon replaced with fear as I begin to understand the message. Or at least I think I do. That phrase—"Speak openly, for I'm your father and you're my son"—was our secret code of sorts. Whenever I was upset or angry, my father would say that to me and remind me that I could tell him anything, that I was free to express my deepest thoughts and feelings—no matter how dark.

*It's a test,* I think, *but for what?*

There's no way my father, the construction laborer, ever could have imagined I would come home for the purpose I have. He was a simple man. He would expect me to grieve his and my mother's death then get on with my life as a doctor. The last thing he'd expect was for me to come home to fight in the resistance. So...is *that* the answer? *Because you died.* That must be it. It's the only reason I'd ever find myself standing here with the key to his safe-deposit box.

I take a shallow breath and open my mouth to speak. The words come slowly. "I've...come home because..." I freeze. Something is wrong. I know in my gut this isn't the answer. *This is a test.* If the answer were so obvious, my father would have left me the password in his written will. But he didn't. Which means he wasn't sure what my motives would be.

*That's it!*

He wants a genuine answer. My father is asking me why I have come. He wants an honest answer. He wants a true answer.

Now my fear turns to panic. If I answer honestly, I'll commit treason in the presence of a bank official. And while the Kingdom hasn't formally seized the banks, they're pretty much under its direct control. Jude could have me sent north for simply uttering the words.

He interrupts my thoughts. "You must finish the sentence. Now."

I probe Jude's eyes. *What sort of man are you?*

I start to finish my sentence but find there's a lump in my throat. I swallow. My hands are shaking again. Twice in one day. But this time it's not anger ricocheting through me—it's horror.

My father's voice echoes in my mind. *Speak openly…my son.*

My father was a straight talker and an honest man. He wants to know why I've come home. I decide to tell him the truth.

"I have come home…to *fight*. I have come home to avenge your death. I have come home to liberate our people in the name of the one true God."

Jude's eyes widen, as if he's seen a ghost. Then he turns sharply on his heel and hurries over to box number forty and inserts both keys. He returns with the metal box and sets it on the wooden table. I watch as he carefully opens the lid, without looking inside, then backs slowly away from the table. My eyes follow him like a mouse dropped in a snake's cage. He is predator and I am prey.

The words I've uttered are punishable by death. I fully expect Jude to inform me that he'll be contacting the Centurion Guard. Or he'll dash out of the room, which will communicate the same thing. I expect him to do something. But he doesn't. Instead he crosses his arms and nods.

When it's clear he won't immediately condemn me, I approach the table gingerly and ask, "Aren't you supposed to leave me alone to do this sort of thing?"

"Please look inside the box."

He unfolds his arms and settles onto the heels of his feet. *Good.* If he's here with me, then he's not out there telling the Kingdom I should be hanged as a traitor. I look again at the box. The lid is open, and I discover a piece of black felt on top of the contents. I reach down, lift the cloth, and discover what's inside.

Nothing.

I spin around to face Jude, but he's not where he was moments before. I crane my head and spin around quickly, surveying the tiny room. No Jude—Jude is gone.

"Wait...Jude?"

I look confusedly back at the table. *What am I missing?* I lift the metal box and run my hand along the inside, using my fingers to probe every inch of its contours. The lining is soft and feels like suede, but it's empty as a drum. I turn the box over and shake it in my hands. Nothing falls out. I inspect the bottom, thinking there might be some engraving or other kind of marking or message. But there's nothing. The box is as generic and uniform as it could be. There's simply nothing to discover.

The door behind me opens, and Jude returns.

"I don't get it," I say. "It's empty. Is this some kind of a joke?"

Jude walks purposefully toward me. "Your father knew the Kingdom would come here to inspect his holdings. I assured him the money was safe. The Kingdom's takeover of the banking system isn't yet complete. It would take an executive order from King Charles himself to transfer an individual's funds out of our vault. Safe-deposit boxes, however, are another story. The regulations are far more porous. The reasoning is that safe-deposit boxes—unlike vaults, which store only cash—could be used to hide contraband and are thus subject to search and seizure. Basically the property stored in this room, while safe from private theft, is treated like all other private property, which means the Kingdom can take it whenever it wants."

"I'm sorry, but I have no idea what you're talking about."

Jude puts a hand on my shoulder, and I can't help notice how small his hands are; they're the hands of a young girl. "The item your father left for you is in a different box," he says. "There were, of course, a few belongings in this original box." Jude points to the table. "But the Centurion Guard seized them, just as your father expected they would."

"Centurions came here? They opened this box? But…how did they know the password?"

Jude laughs and puts his other hand on my opposite shoulder. "The password wasn't for them; it was only meant for *you*. And yes, they came here and demanded to see the box. I showed it to them, and they took the contents with them."

"What was in it?"

"Nothing of value," Jude says casually. He takes his little hands off me and puts them in his pockets, which I appreciate. "A few collectors' coins. I think they were old US currency—quarters and dimes and some other worthless junk. Maybe a few dollar bills? I can't recall. The box was worth a thousand Worlds…at most. Chump change to you, rich boy."

"Why would my father think the Kingdom would come to steal his property?"

"He didn't think—he *knew!* And his prediction was dead-solid perfect."

"My father laid brick for forty years," I say, feeling my blood pressure rise, my body heat rolling out from underneath my collar. I turn away from Jude. "He learned to read and understand basic arithmetic before dropping out of school. My mother had even less of an education. They were simple people. This must be some sort of…*misunderstanding*."

"There's a lot you don't know about your parents, Deacon."

I turn around. "Like what?"

"Let's start with your opening the box your father left for you—the real one, the box he wanted you to see, if you were up to it."

"You have the key?"

Jude pulls two small keys from his pocket. "After you gave me the correct password, I had you open the empty box so you'd know I can be trusted."

"I don't know that."

Jude smirks. "You will soon." He walks briskly to the corner of the room and opens box number seven. He retrieves the box, carries it to the table, and places it next to box forty. He opens it and steps back, just as he did before. "Take a peak," he teases.

I eye Jude suspiciously before approaching the table. Just like before, a black cloth covers the contents. I toss it aside and, in one cataclysmic moment, realize I never knew my father.

Lying peacefully in the safe-deposit box is the most forbidden of all forbidden possessions.

# CHAPTER 5

I reach inside the box and find a handgun crafted of stainless steel.

This is the first time I've ever touched a gun. I run my fingers along its ridges as a surge of adrenaline springs up my arm and shoots directly into my heart, which responds by pumping furiously inside my chest.

*A gun. And it's not in the hands of a centurion. It's been hiding in this box, waiting... for me.*

The gun's handle is cold and feels much different than I imagined it would. I slip my fingers around the butt and slide a finger onto the trigger. Then I slowly draw it out of its hiding place.

I raise the contraband in front of me and am surprised by its weight, by how wondrously light the thing is. I extend my arm and imagine what it would be like to aim the barrel at the enemy. My arm shakes, and the gun dances small circles before me.

"Careful," Jude says. "It's loaded."

Another rush of adrenaline explodes in my brain. "Loaded?" I say, astonished at the savage thought—at the reality that I'm holding a tool capable of doling out death. With one pull of this trigger, I could...I've never experienced such a high, such a rush of unadulterated possibility. I feel dizzy.

"Yes," Jude says. "Loaded. There are nine bullets in the clip waiting to be pumped into Kingdom sympathizers."

I lower the gun. "You're part of the resistance?"

Jude flinches. "This room isn't monitored, but it's best if we say nothing more."

He collects box forty from the table and returns it to its cubbyhole in the wall. As he slides the box into place, he says, "It's illegal for me to allow someone to retrieve contraband from a safe-deposit box. The penalty for storing is

25

minimal but not for allowing retrieval. Should I, or any other bank employee, permit someone to leave these premises with a banned object, the punishment would be death—for you and me." Jude locks the box in the wall. "Do you understand what I'm saying?"

"I do. But I don't understand why or how this—"

He walks back toward me. "If we stay in this room any longer, it'll raise suspicion. I can answer most of your questions but not now. Right now you need to ensure this gun is hidden when you walk through the lobby."

I take the gun and shove it down the back of my pants and pull my jacket over it, like I've seen outlaws do in the old movies. I turn my back to Jude for inspection.

"Not bad," he says. "Just be sure to hold it securely when you start running."

More adrenaline floods my blood. "Why would I be running?"

"Because there's something I haven't told you."

Jude moves decisively for the door.

"What?" I say. "What haven't you told me?"

"Time to go."

"Jude, what haven't you told me?"

"When you walk out of the bank, the metal detector will sound. But I'm not worried, because you'll get a good jump on the guards."

"The alarm will go off!"

Jude nods. "Yes, of course. Weapons aren't allowed inside the bank. But fortunately for you, the alarm is basically our only line of defense. I don't think you'll have any problem escaping."

*Escaping.* The word hits me hard and fast. "But what about the guards?"

Jude waves his hand as if swatting a bee. "Centurion rejects. Total incompetents. You'll be out the door before the alarm sounds, which will give you the head start you'll need. Since you'll be leaving the bank, the guards won't give chase beyond a few yards. They'll worry it's a trap designed to lure them away from their posts. I'll reassure the guards and my manager that you took nothing from the box, as it was already empty, and then I'll volunteer to file the official report to the Office of Record, which I'll forget to do. That should be the end of it. Just a false alarm. Nothing more and nothing less.

Happens all the time. The Kingdom won't pay much attention to a small bank alarm in Oxford."

The word *escape* bangs around in my head. Half an hour ago, a madwoman was strangling me, and now I'm being asked to smuggle contraband from a Kingdom bank. If my stay in the South keeps up this frenetic pace, I'll be dead before sunset.

I examine Jude carefully. He appears trustworthy…sort of. He seems to have all the answers, but something about him unsettles me, though I can't put my finger on it. If this is an elaborate trap, he's done a convincing job. Perhaps that's exactly what this is—a ruse to have me arrested. Put a gun in my hand, then take me down. My stomach drops at the thought.

"How do I know I can trust you?"

Jude looks me dead in the eyes. "You don't."

"Then why should I?"

"What other choice do you have?"

"I can put the gun back in the safe-deposit box and pretend this conversation never happened," I tell him. "Or I can put this gun to your head and pull the trigger."

"And then what?"

"Do what I came home to do."

"And you're prepared to shoot your way out of here?"

"I'm prepared to do whatever it takes to see the Kingdom overthrown."

Jude sighs. "Do you know how difficult it is to secure a gun in the South?"

I nod, which is a lie. I have no idea.

"That gun gives you power," Jude says. "The real kind."

"To do what? Take on the Centurion Guard with a single handgun and nine bullets? That's ridiculous."

Jude rolls his eyes. "There's so much you don't understand. That gun is your entry into the game. With that gun and your money…don't you see, Deacon? This is the beginning. Right here and right now. The true beginning of the final resistance, the one that will break the Kingdom's back."

"I don't know what you're talking about. All of this…it's a lot to absorb. I thought…well, I don't know what I thought."

Jude steps forward and once again places his weird little hand on my shoulder. "I know. That's why I'm asking you to trust me. Get out of here with that gun, and I promise your questions will be answered. The hopes of an entire people will die right here and now if you're unwilling to take this next step. The South needs you, Deacon." He laughs darkly. "*I* need you."

A voice screams in my head, telling me that if I walk out the bank door with a gun, I won't live to see any of what Jude is talking about. The alarm will sound and that will be the end.

This is a suicide mission.

But another voice tells me this is the moment I've waited for my whole life. The time has come; my decision is made.

"How do I contact you?"

Jude smiles. "You don't. I'll find you."

"How?"

"You're scheduled to meet Miles tonight, correct?"

I arch my eyebrows. "How did you…?"

"See you at the park."

Jude winks and opens the vault door.

# CHAPTER 6

This is the first near-death experience of my life, and so far I hate it. My heart races as I follow Jude out from the safe-deposit room, down the hallway, and back through the red door that leads directly into the bank lobby. Once there, we find two armed men who now have legal cause to arrest me and send me north to the camps or, if Dr. Stone is so inclined, have me shot.

But I'd never be that lucky. From what I know of Dr. Stone, she'd opt for a hanging, which is far more dramatic. And she'd hope my neck wouldn't break so I'd suffer a slow, agonizing death by asphyxiation. I imagine wrapping my hands around *her* neck.

The lunch hour is over, and the lobby is all but empty. Two people are waiting in line for the teller, but other than that, the bank is deserted—except for the guards of course. The steady hum of the airconditioner registers too loudly in my ears. No music plays in the background.

The two guards in the lobby sport Kingdom police uniforms and stand on either side of the bank's doors. Both men brandish guns on their hips, and both glare at Jude and me. Or maybe it's just me?

Jude turns to me and, in an exaggerated voice, says, "I'm sorry we couldn't be of further assistance to you today, Mr. Larsen. But I hope this disappointment won't deter you from continuing to bank with us. We'd hate to lose your business." He smiles and reaches to shake my hand. I smile blankly at him and offer a flimsy shake in return. My legs are noodles, and my stomach feels queasy as we approach the door.

I hold Jude's hand for a moment too long and say, "No problem at all."

I release my sweaty palm and step between the two guards, one of whom moves to open the door for me. He swings the door wide, smiles tightly, and says, "Good afternoon, young man."

"Thanks," I stutter.

There's nothing to do now but walk through the open door. But the rare gesture of kindness from the guard isn't a fortuitous thing. When the alarm sounds, he'll be within reaching distance of me. There's no way for me to slip out the door without him snatching hold of me.

But I have no other option. I swallow hard and walk through the door.

My shoulder brushes the guard's chest, and he says, "May the gods of our Kingdom protect you."

The words have just left his mouth when my fist shatters his nose.

Blood spews brilliantly from the guard's face, but I'm out the door before a drop of it stains the floor. And then I'm gone.

As I tear away from the bank, the sensation of cartilage crunching beneath my hand sends a fresh round of adrenaline through my veins. It's the first time I've inflicted pain on my enemy. During my training I'd wondered whether I could actually do it. Was it in me to torment another human? Would I be capable of…killing? These questions haunted me. I had countless nightmares of traveling home only to discover I was born a coward.

But now I'm baptized, with blood on my hands to prove it.

A dry smile rolls across my face as my legs carry me to safety, or to wherever it is I'm headed. *I've joined the fight!* I'm not a coward. Quite the contrary, I'm a violent man. I feel it deep in my bones.

I make a hard turn and slide around a dusty street corner, taking a moment to look behind me. Jude was wrong. Both guards have given chase. We're separated by less than a hundred yards. Either man could easily gun me down. I consider drawing my weapon and firing at them. The mantra "Kill or be killed" flashes brightly across my brain.

I'm in a full sprint when my brain registers the howl of the bank's alarm. It screams an ear-deafening call to arms for any Kingdom centurion who hears it. This is when the gravity of what I've done sinks in, working to erase the rush of adrenaline. There's no way for me to escape Oxford. Even if I manage to kill both of these men, more will come for me. I've committed one of the most severe crimes—defiance of authority. If that isn't bad enough, if they arrest me, they'll discover my gun. For that offense I'll be assured the slowest and most painful of Kingdom deaths—death on a cross. Getting shot or hanged sounds like a vacation by comparison.

These truths hit me like a cold bucket of water, and my legs fold beneath my body. As I tumble forward, concrete rips the skin off my outstretched hands before my chin collides with the ground and splits wide open.

But the truth burns far worse than the gash on my chin. I've attacked a Kingdom guard...and I'll be executed.

Searing pain fires from my chin into the back of my jaw. But there's no time to afford myself a moment of pity. I use my bloody hands to scramble back to my feet and keep running hard and fast, willing my body to find one final gear of speed.

The streets and the people on them are a blur. The siren wails. The guards close in. I'm a strong runner, but the adrenaline has my heart beating entirely too fast for me to find a sustainable pace. My lungs cry out for oxygen, demanding my legs slow down. A dagger-like pain cuts jaggedly across my chest. My legs are gassed. It's only a matter of seconds before they give out and I'll be back on the ground.

I'm slowing down. My body is crashing. There will be no escape.

I look behind me. There's now only one guard in pursuit, and it's not the one I struck in the face. *Good. If I'm going to die today, at least I made one of them suffer.* This cruel thought gives me a surprising amount of joy in my last moments.

That's when the guard gets down to business. A shot rings out, and the whoosh of a bullet screams past my ear. I hit the ground. In a panic I flip my aching body over and meet the end of a steel barrel.

"Freeze! Don't move!" The guard comes closer and kicks my inner thigh with a tremendous amount of force. "Roll onto your stomach, and place your hands on your back. *Slowly!*"

I do precisely as he says, resting my bloody hands on top of the gun I've concealed beneath my jacket. The guard's boots click-clack against the concrete as he circles me. He speaks breathlessly into his radio, calling for backup. I have only seconds to react.

I make my move the moment he gets close to my legs and not a second later. Kicking out hard, I sweep his boots from underneath him. An errant gunshot cracks out, and the guard falls backward, landing hard on the ground. He tries to retrain his weapon on me, but I'm too fast. Like a silver wolf pouncing on prey, I leap on him and jam my knee hard on his throat.

I reach for my gun and frantically draw it out. Then I dig the barrel hotly into his neck and say, "Drop it."

The guard doesn't obey. Instead he jerks and tries to aim his gun at me. I press down harder on his windpipe, sealing off his air supply. His face turns purple, and he drops his weapon.

Another siren roars out, echoing loudly off the buildings around us. The Centurion Guard is on the way. With my knee firmly in place, I spin my head, desperately searching for a way out. A child's wide eyes watch from an open second-floor window of a shabby midrise apartment building. When our gazes meet, he backs slowly into the shadows of his apartment. He, like everyone else, wants no part of this. The sirens and the noise of a scuffle have sent everyone into hiding, as they rightly should. No need to be present when the authorities come around, as nothing good ever comes of it.

My eyes dance from building to building and dark window to dark window. There's no way out and no one to help. I curse loudly.

I look down at the guard, whose face has turned a ghastly shade of blue. The man needs to breathe, and I need to run. Sweat drips off my bloodied chin and splatters onto his lips. His eyes are bugging out of his head. He'll die soon if I don't let up.

Before I can think better of it, I lift my knee from his throat. He hoarsely draws a gallon of air and immediately chokes on it. He spits up blood.

I lean down close to his face and say, "I came home to kill men like you. Nothing would give me more pleasure than to put this gun to your temple and flick the trigger. Do you understand?"

His voice is raw. "Yeah," he says with a tremble.

"If I hear the Kingdom is looking for a man with a gun, I'll come to your home and kill you, and I won't use this gun. Got me?"

The guard nods his head furiously, eager to comply. Jude was right. This man isn't a hardened centurion; he's a washout, a failure who's terrified of both killing and dying. Unfortunately for him, I fear neither, a truth I know he can see in my eyes.

That's when I'm filled with an unstoppable rage to murder him. He's the epitome of every evil that dominates this country. This guard—this pathetic excuse for a human being—is a cog in the great machine that keeps my people oppressed, only a small step removed from slavery. As long as King Charles reigns, we in the South will never be free.

This man needs to die, and he needs to die now.

I might not get another chance.

# CHAPTER 7

I hear her voice before I see her face.

In a silky and unfamiliar accent, she says, "Don't do it. Come with me. We have only seconds."

I tilt my head toward the soft voice and raise the gun, taking aim at the dark woman from the Office of Record. Her tears are gone, replaced with a dry and resolute stare. I lower my gun and direct it back to the guard lying beneath me. The color of life has returned to his face; his eyes dart wildly, his mind trying to devise a plan.

"Don't even think about it," I tell him. "I dare you to give me the hint of an excuse to pull this trigger."

The sirens are louder now, no farther than a block away. If I stay where I am for another minute, it'll be too late. If the centurions around the corner see me—gun in hand—they'll mow us down.

This girl and me. No questions will be asked; their rifles will simply explode to red-hot life, and then there'll be nothing but the silence of death—but not before the pain.

The young woman, in a breathy whisper, pleads, "Come with me. I'll show you the way."

I have no reason to trust this dark-skinned woman with eyes like the night. "Who are you?" I say, the desperation in my voice startling even to me. It has the timbre of a man drowning.

"No time for that. *Come!*" She offers me her small hand, taking hold of my bloody fingers. "Before it's too late. Before we have no choice."

I look once more at the guard, who now looks hopeful. He knows his brethren will be on us soon, knows I'm a dead man walking. A ghost of a smile

34

flickers across his exhausted face. I practically can hear the hope exploding into his brain.

"I won't use my gun," I remind him. "It won't be quick."

I raise my gun and bring its butt down viciously on the crown of his head, knocking him out cold. The crunching thud of steel against skull is sickening, but I feel no regret for what I've done. He wears the uniform of the men who murdered my parents. It's as simple as that.

Then I'm running again, following closely after this gorgeous stranger as she slips inside a dark high-rise.

She floats like an angel before me, her black hair streaming back and whipping me in the face. I follow frantically behind, praying this place will be our sanctuary. She moves with the confidence of someone familiar with the night and at home in the dark. When I trip and stumble for the third time as we round a blind corner and bound down yet another flight of stairs, she slows her pace and offers me her hand. And that's how we carry on, my hand buried inside hers, gripping it tightly, as if it were life itself—which of course it now is.

We've descended far below street level, yet I can still hear the howl of our pursuers. It's a royal cacophony of panicked sounds: sirens, harsh voices, the shuffling of boots, megaphones, barking dogs—vicious and bloodthirsty.

And then my name. The Centurion Guard is calling out my name. "Deacon Larsen! Halt! Deacon Larsen! Stop running! Give yourself up before it's too late! Halt! In the name of King Charles...surrender!"

"Where are we going?" I say, even more anxious now, only seconds away from capture and torture. We've exited a concrete stairwell into a long corridor that's barely wide enough for two people to traverse. We're still holding hands when we slow to catch our breath. We're both gasping hard for air.

"They won't find us here," she says.

"But they know we came into this building."

"The soldiers will only come so far. Kingdom officials, especially the Guard, will never come all the way down. Not to this cursed place."

We reach the end of the narrow corridor, and I discover it's a dead end. I hear my name called out again, warning me that I must surrender. The voices have grown louder and angrier. I hear the banging of boots and the clatter of men garbed in armor as they bound down steps, taking two and three at a time.

"What now?" I say, turning to this woman who has thrown away her life in a matter of minutes.

She doesn't answer. Instead she presses a dusty button on what looks like a small intercom on the wall. A voice crackles instantly from it. "Who's there?"

"It's Maria," she says, her voice shakier than before.

*Her name is Maria.*

The voice on the other end pauses for far too long. Maria and I share a worried look. Time is running out. The centurions and their dogs are now in the corridor. Flashlights paint our faces alight. German Shepherds scratch and claw against the concrete floor as they hurl their fangs toward us. It'll all be over soon.

Finally an angry voice replies, "What do you want?"

"No time to explain. You must let us in. Please!"

Another pause. Then an impressive unlocking sound clicks, and the wall opens before us, revealing a small elevator with blood-red walls. I grab Maria by the waist and leap into the chamber. We crash hard to the floor. As the doors close, one of the centurions lets loose his dog from the leash. The slobbering beast tears forth and leaps powerfully off his hind legs—teeth out—and slams into the steel doors as they shut, sealing us inside.

The elevator shudders and moves downward.

Under the red glow off the elevator, I regard my new friend. Her face shines with sweat, and I wonder what it would be like to hold her in my arms, to kiss her delicate lips.

"Do you trust me?" she says, her breath shallow and quivering.

"Yes."

"Good," she says soberly. "Because down here…you'll need to."

As the elevator plunges hundreds of feet beneath the earth's surface, the din of barking dogs is replaced by the thick whir of the elevator's machinery—*hummmmmmmmm.*

Down we go.

Then the thumping begins, hard and fast, its pulse infecting my bloodstream like a sticky flu—*Doosh. Doosh. Doosh. Doosh. Doosh.*

I hear it loud and clear long before the elevator finishes its descent. It's a pounding beat, repeating its rhythm over and over, the trance quickly imprinting itself on my brain. When the elevator stops and the doors open, the beat is joined by a bass so bruising that I feel it reverberate in my knees. I've never heard music so loud in my life, if music is even what you call such a noise; it sounds more like an explosion.

Maria grazes a hand across my chin as the doors open. Above the noise she hollers, "Follow me." She offers me her hand, and I take it. "Don't let go!" she orders.

"Never" is what I want to tell her. *I'm never letting you go.* Our hands meld as if they were fashioned from the beginning of time to do so, as if this is all they're good for, to make the other body know the tender touch of love. We've barely shared ten sentences between us, yet I feel as if we've traveled a lifetime by each other's sides—intimately familiar with how the other moves, breathes, *wants.* I cling to her as if she were my only purchase in this world, the one true thing I can grasp. I long to touch more of her.

Maria guides me out of the elevator purposefully, her eyes focused ahead on some unknown target, a destination I can't imagine. My eyes dart this way and that, my mind manically doing its best to process the imagery my senses feed it. But it's maximum overload, and despite my best efforts, I can't absorb this dark circus in its entirety. I catch only vignettes, my attention divided between my surroundings and my need to stay as close to Maria as possible.

The space is damp and cold. My initial guess is that we're in an abandoned underground railway. The walls are a dark brick, and they're covered in a slippery film that shines like oil. I smell a putrid mixture of mildew, stale tobacco, and vomit. I reflexively lean closer to Maria and inhale the vanilla of her jet-black hair.

We walk at an even clip. The bass continues to thump at an unholy decibel, and my eyes slowly adjust to the absolute darkness of this buried place. To my immediate right is the brick wall, but to my left is what feels like a cavernous space. I squint and confirm my initial guess was correct. I make out a deep divide and can just barely decipher the steel railing running along the base of the depressed floor.

I put my mouth near Maria's ear, my lips grazing her skin, and ask, "What is this place?"

Maria shakes her head. "You don't want to know."

"Why won't the centurions come down here?"

Maria makes a sharp right turn, and we hurry up a small set of stairs that leads through an archway that's slightly better lit than the first room. That's when I begin to understand.

The hallway is filled with people. There must be hundreds of them. They're filthy, their faces smudged in grease, their foreheads shiny with alcohol-laden sweat. The smell in the hallway is infinitely worse, and no amount of vanilla in Maria's hair can prevent the stench from invading my nostrils.

Our pace is dramatically slowed as we snake through the overcrowded space. The farther we travel, the louder the music gets, growing to a deafening crescendo. I can't understand how anyone could stand being in here for any length of time. My head aches.

*Doosh. Doosh. Doosh. Doosh. Doosh.* I fear it will never end.

No one bothers to glance our way as we pass; they appear lost in their individual worlds. I don't hear a single person speaking to another, not that I could with the noise, but still it's severely unsettling to see this many people jammed into a small space with no one appearing interested in anyone else. It's almost as if they can't see one another.

That's when the penny drops. These people aren't in their right minds.

A girl who must be several years younger than me is leaning against the wall. Her eyes catch mine. She has fiery irises, and she smiles wildly as her fingers unfurl from a syringe. She drops the needle, and her eyes roll back into her head.

The seizure starts after that.

I stare wide-eyed at the young girl who has just fallen to the mossy floor. She has collapsed into the fetal position, and her seizure has stopped. I fear she's dead. I move toward her to help, but she's enveloped into a fold of men who lunge and grope for her discarded needle. I stumble backward, tripping as I try to escape the scene. I turn and stroke my arms over people as though swimming through rough ocean waves. Each person I shove past stares at me with open eyes that do not see.

I find Maria in the thick crowd, her dark skin standing out among the ashen faces. I grab hold of her shoulder and demand an answer. "What is this place? Where are we?"

She keeps moving, her eyes focused on a destination beyond the mass of people. "We're almost there," she says quickly. "I promise. But we *must* keep moving. It's not safe...especially here. These people are cannibals. They'll eat us alive—and savor every bite."

We carry on like this for at least another two hundred yards, bobbing and weaving, pushing where we must, until the cohesive glob of humanity begins to break apart and there's finally room to draw a breath of air untainted by human waste.

I inhale deeply and catch Maria's sweet smell once more. It's enough to keep me moving.

Maria continues to walk with a confidence that suggests she knows this dungeon well. We take a decisive left out of the crowded hallway and pass through another archway that's guarded on either side by two men wearing long black robes with hoods. Neither seems to have a weapon, but my body tenses just the same, preparing for the fight I know is coming; I feel it in my bones.

The passageway is narrow, with room for only one person at a time. Maria leads the way. Neither hooded man moves as she passes, and while I can't see either face from beneath the shadows of their hoods, both men issue snakelike hisses as I brush past their shoulders. I'm narrowly beyond these men, if that's what they are, when a long hand reaches out from the robe and scrapes my arm with the sharp claw of a wolf.

I jump forward as blood flows down my arm. The passageway is pitch black, and I walk blindly, clutching to Maria for guidance. While the absence of light makes for an even more terrifying journey, here—in this tunnel that feels like a crypt—we find our first respite from the deafening roar of the techno beat. With each step we venture into the abyss, the noise settles deeper in the recesses of the awful place we've left behind. The silence, however, is a small consolation for the growing dread of walking into a black hole.

Maria whispers to me as we shuffle along, "How is your head? You took quite a fall."

*My head.* I've all but forgotten the episode with the bank guard. I reach around to feel that my gun is still secure in the waistband of my pants. The adrenaline from our escape suppressed any pain I might have felt, but now it blossoms to painful life on my chin and deep within the sockets of my jaw. I pat my face with my bruised hand and feel that my jaw has begun to swell. I stick a dirty finger into the gash on my chin; it's sticky and warm with blood.

"I'm fine," I say. "It's nothing I can't clean myself."

"Nonsense," she says. "I'll bandage you after we speak with Legion."

"Who's Legion?" I say.

"You'll find out soon."

"Wait. Who are you…and why are you helping me? You saved my life."

Maria stops walking and turns her body to face mine, wrapping her arms tightly around my waist. It's supremely dark, and I can't see the face I know is within inches of my own. I feel her sweet breath on my lips, and my body trembles. She presses her chest against mine and resurrects the part of me I thought was dead forever—my heart.

"I saw you," she says into my ear. "In the Office of Record, when I was crying."

"Yes," I say, anxious for her to know. "I saw you too. You were beautiful. You…are beautiful."

"I applied for a northern visa. It took two years to process." Maria pauses, and the darkness feels as if it's spreading out around us. We're like two people floating in infinite space, with only each other to hold onto. "Today it was denied."

I run my hand across her face and feel tears stream down her cheeks. "Why do you want to go north? It only makes it easier for them to enlist you in the camps."

"The West is off limits for a foreigner like me. And I'll do anything to escape the South. It's my only hope for a new life. Or at least it was." Maria's hands are now on my face, her fingers exploring my nose and lips. "But then I saw you. I can't explain it. Your eyes…they were so gentle, so…kind. You cared about my pain. I saw it in your eyes."

"My eyes told you that?" I whisper. "If you hadn't been there, just now on the street, I'd...I'd be dead. No doubt about it. You risked your life to save me. How do you thank a person for something like that?"

Maria kisses my forehead, and I can no longer feel the ground beneath my feet. We're fully suspended in the darkness of space, our bodies pressed together as one.

"Where have you been?" I say, fumbling for the words to express my ineffable heart.

"In places I pray you'll never go."

"I'm here now. Wherever you've been, Maria, whatever you've suffered, that's over now. I can take you away from this place. I'll get you out of the South."

"Tell me your name," she says.

"Deacon. And you have me now, and it's all you'll need."

Maria stiffens, and I fear she can see straight through me, understanding how preposterous my pledge is. I want it to be true, and maybe I even believe it will be true. All these feelings are so new, so unexpected. I'm speaking without thinking first.

But the truth is I haven't come home to fall in love. I've come home to fight in a war, and my destiny will take me north, if I live that long. And when I go north, I won't be traveling with a lover. I'll be marching with other warriors, men prepared to fight and die for the cause. It's foolish and unfair for me to promise Maria freedom and safety. Yet I can't bring myself to recant my promise. I want it too dearly.

"Maria?" I say. "Do you believe me?"

Before she can answer, a blast of cold air rushes toward us. The hair on my neck and arms prickles to attention. Then a voice, which can be described only as infernal, slithers out from the dark.

"Welcome home, Maria."

# CHAPTER 8

I push Maria behind me, shielding her from whatever lurks in the abyss. "Who's there?" I say.

My question is answered with the laugh of a madman.

"He calls himself 'Legion,'" Maria says quietly. "But his real name is Alejandro. We must talk to him. Alejandro controls access to the tunnel, the only way out of here. He's also one of the reasons the Centurion Guard won't venture too far underground."

"He's that dangerous?"

"Every bit," Maria says. "He killed three centurions last month—by himself."

"He has weapons?"

"He doesn't need them. He killed all three with nothing but his hands. But his army does have weapons—weapons not even the centurions possess."

"His army?" I say, certain I've misunderstood her.

"Yes. Alejandro controls an army of a thousand men."

I can't imagine how an unarmed man could take down a single centurion yet alone three of them. Centurions are the most well-trained soldiers on the planet. Their lethality is legendary. What's even harder to understand is how a man living hundreds of feet below ground has managed to assemble an army.

I'm suddenly eager to meet Alejandro. I say, "Well...that might be a good thing actually."

"No, it's not good. Nothing about what has become of Alejandro is good."

"But he's built an army to resist the Kingdom. How can that not be good?"

"You want nothing to do with him," Maria says flatly.

"Why not?"

"Because it's not the Kingdom that Alejandro's interested in warring against."

"But I thought you said the Kingdom was afraid of him. I've never heard of the Guard backing down from anyone. I was under the impression the Kingdom controlled every region of the South, afraid of no man."

"They do…and they aren't. This underworld is the single stronghold left in the South. The Kingdom leaves Alejandro and his men completely alone, as if they have some sort of unspoken deal."

"Just because he managed to kill a few mercenaries?"

"No," Maria whispers. "Because they share a common enemy."

Alejandro's voice rolls forth from the void. "I've been waiting for you."

A fresh chill dances up my spine.

"What do you want me to do?" I ask.

"Precisely as he says."

"What if I don't?"

"You don't want to know."

"You keep saying that."

Maria leans close to me, and I smell the lavender on her skin. She says, "You said you'd trust me."

"That was before I knew about Alejandro."

"He won't harm us."

"What…is he?" I say.

"Just a man," Maria says sadly. "Just…a sick man in need of a doctor."

"How do you know all of this?"

"Because," she says, her voice choking on the vinegar of a bitter memory, "Alejandro was my husband."

A harsh light bursts forth, momentarily blinding us. It lasts for only a second before vanishing. Then a much softer light slowly illuminates the cave we've entered. The walls are craggy, and the air is frigid, without a trace of the heavy humidity from the surface above. It's like we've journeyed down into an entirely different world.

Alejandro stands in the center of the circular space with his arms wide, as if we're lost friends returning home from a perilous journey. Like the men guarding the entryway, whom I suspect are demon possessed, Alejandro wears a dark robe. His hood is pulled over his head and casts a shadow across his face. I can't see what he looks like.

As we draw closer, I regard Alejandro's formidable size and surmise that he's nothing short of an absolute building. He's not an inch below seven feet; his shoulders are wide; and his legs look more like tree trunks than mortal limbs. If there was ever a man who could handle three centurions, it's Alejandro.

Maria and I stop walking, keeping our distance from Alejandro. We've finally arrived at our destination. It's odd, but I feel strangely safe in the presence of this dark figure.

Without warning, a guttural noise springs out of Alejandro, reminding me of a wild pig being led to slaughter. It's a nauseating cacophony of what it must sound like to hear the angel of death strangling life from a person not ready to surrender his soul. When he's finished emitting this unholy tumult, he says, "This took longer than I'd expected. But I knew you'd be back."

"I'm not back, Alejandro," Maria says curtly. "We're just passing through. We need access to the tunnel. I need you to give it to us."

I'm lifted from my feet and sent flying backward at a hundred miles an hour. My back slams violently against the sharp angles of the craggy wall, and pain explodes throughout my body. A force I can't see or fight keeps me paralyzed against the wall, suspended a good ten feet above the cave's floor. Then, slowly, a pressure builds on my chest. It feels like a boulder has been set atop me. I try to speak, but I can't; I'm being crushed to death.

Calmly Alejandro says to Maria, "You should call me 'Legion.'"

Maria runs to me and tries to pull me down from the wall, but it's useless; I'm trapped within an invisible body cast. My head pounds from the lack of oxygen. I have maybe thirty seconds, at best, before I lose consciousness.

Realizing there's nothing she can do for me, Maria turns back to Legion and says, "Let him down! He's done nothing to you! Please!"

Legion laughs, his voice turning another shade darker. "Where did you find this one, Maria? Did the Teacher send him? He's quite green."

"I won't answer a single question until you let him down. There's no reason to hurt him."

My brain begins to slide offline. Maria's voice takes on an underwater hush, making it hard to understand her garbled words.

Legion says, "Are you still following the Teacher?"

"Release him, and I'll tell you anything you want to know. *Please…Legion.*"

"We are many now," he says, sounding pleased Maria has addressed him by the proper name.

"Legion, please, he needs to breathe. *He'll die!*"

Legion flicks his head, and I drop to the ground. The weight is immediately lifted from my chest. I roll onto my back and fill my lungs with cold air, which shocks my throat as it descends into my body. I try to stand, but my body buckles beneath me, and I fall to the ground. Every ounce of strength has been drained from my body. I roll onto my back and suck air. I feel like I've run a hundred miles.

Maria returns her attention to Legion. "We need to travel through the tunnel. This man is wanted by the Centurion Guard, and we can't go back the way we've come."

"Has the Teacher lived up to your lofty expectations?" Legion says, ignoring her question about the tunnel.

Maria draws a deep breath and steels herself for whatever is coming next. Finally she says, "He shattered them…if you want to know the truth."

Legion laughs. "I knew it. No man will ever accept you, not after what you've done. You'll never be clean in the eyes of a man. You're dirty and worthless."

With warm eyes, Maria says, "He shattered them with acceptance. The Teacher treats me like all the others—no different. We're friends."

"What does he demand in return?"

"Nothing," Maria says. "He asks only that we continue following the way."

Legion laughs harder. "What way is that?"

"I'm still learning."

"Then why do you follow?"

"You know what I used to be. You saw my torment." Maria steps closer to Legion. "Look in my eyes now and see the difference." Legion grunts and turns his back to her. "He still asks about you," she says. Legion emits another sound that comes directly from the pits of hell. "You can have this too, Alejandro," she says tenderly, taking a few more steps closer to him. "You don't have to live this way. There's life outside this cave. Turn around and see the difference."

Without turning, Legion says, "This man who accepts you and makes all you rejects hopeful will soon be knocked off his throne. Then what will you be left with? Who will protect you?"

"The Teacher has no throne, nor does he want one."

"We all want a throne!" Legion barks. "And yes, he sits on a throne. But not for long."

Maria takes another bold step toward him and places her tiny hand on his wide back. She looks like a child standing next to him. I scramble weakly to my feet and prepare to lunge at him.

"What are you planning to do?" she asks Legion.

"Stay and find out."

"You know I can't do that," Maria says.

"Can't...or won't?"

"Look at me," Maria says.

To my great surprise, Legion obeys, turning slowly to face Maria.

*He listens to her.*

"Leave this place," Maria says. "Come with us to the park. It's never too late to start over. It doesn't have to be this way. You have the power to change your life."

There's a pregnant pause before Legion responds. It's the sort of silence that can exist only between two people with a lengthy and storied past. It's a pause that holds a thousand words, a thousand memories, and a thousand heartaches. It's a pause that makes me insanely jealous.

Finally Legion says, "The tunnel is yours. Go."

"Legion, you should come—"

"*Go!*" he roars. "Before I change my mind and throw you both to the wolves."

Maria moves quickly around Legion, and I follow after her, but he strikes me hard on the chest, stopping me in my tracks. "Boy," he says slowly, "the next time we meet will be the last day of your life."

I slowly back away from him and allow Maria to lead the way to the tunnel. When we arrive, it appears to be better lit than Legion's cave and similar to the first space we entered. A line for a railway track cuts down the center.

As we make our way through the tunnel, Legion's threat echoes in my head. If another man had uttered those words, I'd have attacked him right there and then. But Legion possesses dark powers. I've come home for a fight—make no mistake about it—but I want no part of that. I came here to fight men...not monsters.

Maria hurries me along for another hundred yards before she slows down. "I'm sorry for what happened in there," she says. "Are you OK?"

"It'll take more than a giant freak with anger issues to stop me."

Maria laughs, and her voice is throaty and full. It's a laugh I want to hear many more times, a laugh I'll work hard to earn.

She intertwines her fingers with mine. "Alejandro was always a jealous man," she says, "even before he became as he is now. He'd fly off the handle if a man so much as looked at me sideways. He was always crazy like that. But I've never seen him show that kind of aggression so quickly. And his powers are clearly growing. He detested you the moment you entered the cave."

"I tend to have that effect on people."

She laughs again. It's even better the second time.

Maria grins. "Not on me."

This time I laugh. "Just give me time. I'll drive you all kinds of crazy."

Maria smiles widely, gazing at me in a way I never dreamed a beautiful woman would. Looking at her is like having bright electricity course through my veins. It's the cardinal energy of men who topple empires, liberate slaves, and move mountains. She's a drug so potent that I already know I'll stop at nothing to get it. It's taken no more than an hour to find myself irrevocably hooked on Maria.

In fact I've been so enmeshed in our conversation that I haven't paid any attention to our walk, making the waiting train seem as if it's materialized from thin air. A man stands on the back deck of the caboose with his arms folded, watching us grimly as we approach. He wears the cap of an engineer, the black bill listing far to the left. His mustache is thick and covers the entirety of his mouth; I wonder how he manages to eat.

The caboose is attached to a single compartment, and the engineer motions for us to climb aboard. We ascend the short ladder and crawl into an empty shipping container that smells of ammonia and bleach. We slide across the floor until our backs are flat against the wall. There are no seats inside.

"You've done this before?" I say.

Maria laughs as our train heaves and lurches forward. "Relax," she says. "We made it. You're safe now."

Without asking, she takes my aching hands into hers and blows gently on them. Her touch is simple yet intimate in ways I've never known. My mother's touch carried with it the magic of solace, but this is different—*very* different. It's both calming and exhilarating. Somewhere deep in my soul—too deep for me to draw fully into the light—I'm aware that my life is changing. Instinctively I know I'll look back on this moment and think, *There. Right there.*

Maria licks her thumb and rubs dried blood from my chin. "This needs to be stitched up."

"I don't mind a scar."

"Do you have many?"

"Scars?"

She nods.

I nod.

"Where?" she says, sliding her body closer to mine, our hipbones touching each other.

"They're the kind you can't see."

She nods again.

The train gathers speed, and I feel a sense of peace knowing we're moving out of this dark place. I peer out the open door of the container and spot small pairs of lights running along the walls. I point to them. "What are those lights for?"

Maria presses her body so close to mine that I feel her heart thumping in her chest. She whispers, "They aren't lights. They're eyes."

# CHAPTER 9

T he tunnel walls resemble a country night's sky; there are thousands of brilliantly shining stars. But they're not exploding balls of hydrogen; they're eyes, and not the kind you want watching over you from the heavens. These eyes have the cold, sharp glow of demons, and they can only mean one thing—the Evil One has seen you; he knows you exist, and he will come for you.

I run my hand across Maria's knee and fantasize about caressing her thigh. "I don't believe in these creatures." I say. "Or at least I didn't. I thought they were a figment created for children. A monster under the bed to scare little ones into minding their parents."

Maria sighs. "It turns out the creatures under the bed are real."

"How did you get mixed up in this? I can't imagine you living down here. You're nothing like those people."

"You didn't know me then. I thank God for that."

"Yes, but…" I start to ask her about Legion, but a lump gathers in my throat where my question belongs. The answer, no matter what it is, will devastate me. If she's still married to that man, I'll die. But she can't be, right? Alejandro is simply…not human. Not anymore.

But they *were* married. She said the words. Maria loved him once, and perhaps she still does. I can't bear the thought of it. I've never felt such radical jealousy. All I know is I want Maria, and I want her to myself.

"I'm not married to him anymore," she says, as if reading my hot thoughts. "Alejandro was a good man, a very good man. But he—*we*—got involved in a way of life we never should have. The fall from grace is easier to come by than one thinks." Maria cries softly as she speaks, the memories like sharp barbs in her brain, injecting each word with pain.

"You don't have to talk about it. It's all behind you."

"No," she says thickly. "I want to tell you. I'd rather it be me than one of the others in the park. I know how they like to talk."

"I don't understand."

Maria speaks slowly, deliberately; she seems sad but not ashamed. "The way Alejandro is now is how I used to be."

It's an incomprehensible idea, the notion that precious and petite Maria could ever resemble anything close to the nightmare that is Legion. "Not possible," I say. "You couldn't possibly—"

"But I was," she says. "Not as powerful, no, but I was cruel, angry, and... *dark*. We both entangled our souls in the dark arts, and I...we...*I* lost control. It's as stupidly simple and pathetic as that. We needed a refuge," she says matter-of-factly. "*Badly*. Alejandro was always a gentle spirit, but his work ethic was never that of a respectable man. He was lazy, and we were drifters. A few months here and a few more there...wherever. Alejandro did manual labor, and I sang in cafés." A trace of a smile flashes across her face. "I had a lovely voice, and it was fine for a time. We preferred transiency to a conventional life. We adored the freedom. But the Kingdom's invasion of the South changed everything. Because of his size, Alejandro was drafted into the Kingdom's foreign army. A month later his orders came in. He would be sent across the sea, and we'd never see each other again. That's when we opened ourselves to...other possibilities."

The train lurches hard as the incline of our ascent grows steeper. We're traveling much faster than I'd expected on this old line. I take another look through the doorway and discover the eyes of the demons have disappeared, their muted effervescence replaced with nothing but darkness. I'm growing tired of the dark but prefer it to the spying eyes of those wretched creatures hiding beneath its cover.

"Those in the underground," Maria says, "granted us asylum from the Kingdom. But we soon discovered their hospitality came at a high price. Before we knew it, we'd lost control of our lives."

"So you were both...what? Possessed?"

"Seven times—for me, that is. It was more for Alejandro. I...can't explain it. The torture is inexplicable. It's like hell itself has taken residence inside your body, in your spirit. I hated myself, and I wanted to die."

"How did you escape? How did you defeat them?"

"I didn't."

"I don't understand."

"I was saved."

"How?"

Maria smiles as a soft beam of light splashes into the train. The car levels out, and the train slows down. She stands and says, "You're about to find out."

The train rolls into the park and stops at a makeshift station consisting of a single bench and a battered sign that reads, GETH PARK. I stand and take Maria's hand as she moves toward the open door. "We're here," she says. "Time for you to meet the Teacher."

"Won't the Kingdom look for me here? I'm a wanted man. And…Maria, I'm afraid you are too. That bank guard saw you; he heard your voice. Nothing will be the same for you now; we're in serious trouble."

"It's a possibility, yes," she admits casually, as if discussing the chances of evening rain showers. "Which is why we must find the Teacher as soon as possible. He'll know what we should do. Don't worry," she says with a wink. "I was hoping nothing was going to be the same."

That does it. I would abandon the war and run away with Maria, should she ask me to. Her dark eyes light my own with a force so potent that I could forget everything but her. We could escape to Mexico, return to whatever small town she's from, and live peacefully by the sea. I could forget the oppression of my people. I could maybe even release the memory of my parents—with time. We could simply vanish and hold each other forever. We could drop all these burdens and leave them for someone else to carry.

I could do this.

*I think.*

I return Maria's wink. "Whatever you say."

The sun is setting as we crawl off the train, the sky a magnificent blend of flaming oranges and soft purples. The air is sweet with magnolia blossoms. The beauty creates a calm in me that couldn't be more opposite than the feelings of dread, fear, and terror I've experienced today. I close my eyes and inhale a deep breath of fresh, warm air. It swirls in my lungs before plunging into my soul, where it does the real life-giving work.

I open my eyes and take in my surroundings. The park is dense with Lacey oaks, trees native to my homeland. Despite the intensity of the summer's heat and the severe lack of rain, the leaves are a rich green due to the oaks' ability to survive drought and high temperatures. Complementing the oaks are large collections of wild shrubs that explode with vibrant colors, making the park an exotic sea of yellows, greens, browns, blues, and pinks.

The landscape is small rolling hills upon which groups of people are gathered. Some sit on wooden benches; others lounge lazily on the ground, their backs flat against the warm earth. All of them, I notice, are smiling, laughing, and enjoying one another's company on this serene evening. This park is a happy place, and it reminds me of the South I hail from—the one I thought had been erased by the presence of the Kingdom and its Centurion Guard.

But it hasn't been erased. It still exists, if only in this small, hidden oasis between the trees. "This is wonderful," I say to Maria.

I'm grateful to finally find myself in a space that feels like home—home, as I've known it only in my dreams for the past three years. Home, as I remember it in the quiet corners of my heart and my mind. Home, as I experienced it as a child whose parents loved him and cared for him.

Maria, too, fills her lungs with the clean air then exhales. "I found truth in this park," she says, lost in a delightful memory I hope she'll tell me about when the time is right.

"This park *is* the truth," I say.

"Yes," Maria agrees. "The only question is what you'll do with it, what you'll do *in* it."

"Who are all these people? They don't look like Kingdom loyalists, but they don't strike me as resistance fighters either."

"We're a blended community with no one credo," she says. "This park is open to anyone who wishes to come. No soul is rejected in this place."

"Even the English?" I say, disgusted by the thought of those people in this Southern sanctuary.

"Even the English," Maria says, a tenor of pride in her voice.

This buzzes me with challenge. "I don't understand. Why would anyone from the Kingdom be welcome here?"

"Don't get spiky," she says. "The Teacher's fame has spread tremendously during the past three years. People come from all around to sit at his feet. He also travels but always returns here, to this park, which is near his hometown. There are no secrets with him. He moves openly and without regard to who may be listening. In one city I saw resistance fighters, American religious authorities, and the Centurion Guard all in his audience, listening intently to his stories. It's an astonishing sight to behold."

"And they all enjoy his teaching?"

"Oh, no!" Maria gasps. "Not at all. Some do of course, but he outrages many, which is why he's grown so popular. He teaches, they say, 'as one with authority.'"

"Why hasn't he been arrested? I'm shocked the Kingdom would allow it."

"There have been many close calls—many. Yet he remains a free man." Maria shrugs. "It's a mystery."

"But he's sympathetic to the cause?"

"Which cause is that?" she asks.

"The cause of the South and the American resistance, the cause of our religion, the cause of the one true God." Righteous anger drenches my voice. "*My cause.*"

"You've come here to fight?" Maria says, clearly stunned by the bruising nature of this truth.

I want to kick myself. Of all the ways to tell Maria, this is the worst. I had hoped to tell her about my parents, to explain I had no choice but to travel home and avenge their deaths. She would understand that. She would see this is the right thing for me, as a son, to do. On the train ride, I nearly spat it all out. I nearly confessed my motives, but then she poured out her past to me, bonding us together. How could I tell her I only came home to die?

I can't look at her; I'm so ashamed. I gaze at the hill closest to us and see a black man with long dreadlocks pouring wine from a large bottle. He smiles and raises the bottle of red in my direction. I look away.

"Yes," I say, hanging my head low. "I came home to fight."

Maria wipes a stray tear from her cheek. "The gun," she says. "I should have known. That's why you were being chased." She stiffens. "What have you done, Deacon? Are you a bandit, a rebel?"

Maria's dark eyes laser me critically, questioning everything about me, probing my face as if I'm a monster charged with a heinous crime.

"Yes," I mumble, "but I've done nothing wrong. Not yet. The gun was given to me. I had no choice but to run from the guards."

Maria's eyes are glassy and removed. She's already placing a veil between us; I feel our connection being disrupted, the innate line of communication destroyed.

I can't let this happen.

"So…what now?" she says. "Will you join that snake pit of conspirators who plot death beneath the stars? Is that what you want? Is that who you are, Deacon? Another angry man thirsty for war?"

"I don't know who I am," I say in a panic. "But why are you so dogmatic about this? You don't understand how complicated it all is."

Maria puts her nose in my face. "Oh, yes, I do! Don't you *dare* try to tell me how bad it is. I've known pain you can't imagine."

"Is that right? Then tell me. Explain away!"

"If I didn't rescue you in the street—*two bloody hours ago*—you'd already be dead. *Muerto*! *Comprende*?"

I start to respond, to yell something back at her but snap my mouth shut. I bite the inside of my cheek. There's no reply. She's right.

"That's how these fights end," Maria says. "With you dead." She pauses then adds, "Every American who comes here hell-bent on war finds himself hanging on a Kingdom cross. All of them. You live by the sword, you die by the sword. It's as uncomplicated as that."

"Not me," I say, chewing hard on my cheek.

"Because you're different?" Maria shakes her head and wipes away more tears. "God! That's what they all say!"

I take her by the shoulders and shake her as I speak. "*I. Am. Different.*"

"Why is that?" she says, her voice frail and brittle. "What makes you so special? What is it that will keep you off that cross?"

"Money. I have a lot of money."

Maria's lips arc downward. "Money can't save you from the Kingdom's cruelty."

"Maybe not," I say, taking her tanned face gently in my hands. "But it can build an army."

Then I kiss her before she can stop me.

I draw Maria into me, and she wraps her arms around my neck, running her fingers through my hair. I kiss her slowly, tasting the salt on her lips. She's only the third woman I've kissed, and my lips tremble with the nerves of naïveté. Maria, who's far more relaxed, opens her mouth wide and bites my bottom lip.

We continue to kiss, exploring the wild landscapes of our faces and mouths for long enough to know we're in love. If our hands had felt designed for one another, this kiss proves the primordial pairing, sealing the fate of our union.

She is mine and I am hers.

For the first time since my parents were killed, I truly reconsider my decision to go to war. For real. Not as some fleeting thought.

I hadn't anticipated Maria in my life. But who could? Everything about her is exquisitely novel and as such changes everything.

When the time is right, we stop kissing and look at each other in the way only new lovers can. We're pristine creatures holding secret knowledge about the other. "What would you suggest I do, if not fight?" I ask her. "If not go to war? What choice do I have? Something must be done to free our people from these tyrants."

"There's another way to freedom. The Teacher speaks of it often."

"Does he support the American cause?"

"Of course, but the Teacher wishes *all* people to be free."

"All people can't be free. Freedom doesn't work that way."

"You were right," Maria says.

"About what?"

"You *are* different. I know it." She moves her fingers gingerly across my chest. "You don't see it now...but you will. You have the eyes to see. It's all about the eyes—about how we choose to see the world."

"See what?" I say, suddenly growing weary from the adventure of the day. The fatigue settles fast across my shoulders like the burden of a heavy yoke.

"I'm not sure I fully understand it all myself, but I'm beginning to, and it's marvelous. It's just...it's all going to be OK."

"That doesn't answer my question."

"I'm sorry," Maria says, grinning. "That's the best I can do for now. I can't put it in words. But I will."

"I need you to. I want to understand what you're talking about."

"Then you'll have to ask the Teacher yourself." Maria jumps and points at something behind me. "There! I see Jude. They're coming now." She grabs hold of my face. "Now kiss me again."

"Jude! The bank teller?"

Maria laughs playfully and kisses my ear. "Have you met him?"

"Uh...*yeah*! I absolutely cannot—"

Maria's lips are on me before I can finish my sentence. And then there's nothing in the world but her mouth kissing mine.

# CHAPTER 10

Someone calls Maria's name, and I turn to see a group of men marching merrily toward us. They're a motley crew of unmerited bravado. They come in all shapes and sizes and are horribly disheveled, even by poverty-induced Southern standards. The men are unshaven, and their clothing is old and wrinkled. One of them is barefoot. If I didn't know better, I'd take these men for a gang of vagabonds.

Which might be exactly what they are.

But the expression on their faces is anything but the gnarled look of the seriously poor. These men smile and laugh wildly as they walk, their faces brightly lit with mirth. Their happy voices roll out before them like trumpets announcing their arrival.

Only one man in the group doesn't smile, and it's Jude.

I avert my eyes and regard the others. I'm shocked to see another face I know…Miles, the cab driver. He laughs loudly, and his white teeth contrast marvelously against his black skin. All the men look happy, but Miles stands out. He walks with the enthusiastic bounce of a child tramping his way through a forest of make-believe.

I count twelve men in total and pray these men don't represent the true resistance. *This can't be them; these men aren't fighters.*

"These are your friends?" I say.

Maria watches the men with pride. "The best I've ever had. They're my brothers now."

Panic floods my chest, but I manage to say, "A brother to you…is a brother to me." I drape my arm around her shoulder and pull her close. Just touching her skin staves my fear and makes me wonder how I lived a day without her. No matter what disaster lies ahead, at least I've found her.

Maria's "brothers" arrive. One of them breaks away from the group and runs to meet us. Maria lets go of me and rushes to the man with open arms. He lifts her in the air and swings her around as if she's a child, both of them laughing like school kids on summer vacation. Maria's still wearing the dress from her meeting at the Office of Record, and it fans out like a sail as she twirls gracefully through the air. Eventually the gregarious man sets her down. Then the others take turns hugging her and take their time doing it. Some of them kiss her on the cheek.

I don't like these brothers very much.

These men know Maria; they share bonds and memories I'm not privy to. The thought of it drives me wild, which I know is unreasonable. But I can't help it. I've never felt this way before.

These men are so ecstatic to see Maria that I recognize at once how inexplicably bound to this ragtag team she is. I'm clearly not the only man who understands her value. This sets off an alarm in my head, but I do my best to ignore it.

The men file past me, one by one, and introduce themselves. They're kind and polite, each man saying he's been eager to meet me. I'm taken aback by their enthusiasm—and their knowledge of me—and can offer only a simple "Thank you" in return. I try to keep up with the names, but beyond Miles and Jude, I catch only a "John" and a "Lucas."

Miles greets me with a bear hug. "I see you've met our Maria!" he practically screams. He sets me down and wags a long finger. "Behave yourself with her, young man. We're quite the protective group of big brothers. She's our *princesa*, and we're her *caballeros*. Isn't that right, boys?"

The men cheer in affirmation.

Jude has waited to greet me last. We shake hands firmly. He leans close to my ear and whispers, "What in the name of the gods was that stunt about?"

Through clenched teeth I say, "I reacted to the situation. It's not like you gave me time to prepare."

"I told you to walk out of the bank, not start a war in the streets. You could have gotten us both killed."

"I did what I thought was best. Are they searching for Maria and me?"

Jude pulls away. Up ahead the group has begun to drift farther into the park. Maria has joined them, walking arm in arm with one of the guys whose name I can't remember. We move slowly in their direction but linger back so we can speak in private.

"No," Jude says. "I told the bank manager about your parents. Explained that you're a distraught kid who's already being watched closely by the Kingdom. Lucky for you, I convinced him not to file a report with your supervisor at the Office of Record. I had to call in all my favors to avoid it. You broke that guard's nose. The other one has a concussion, says he barely remembers what happened."

"Thank you," I say.

"Men have been hanged for much less than you did today."

"I know."

"If you're going to survive long enough to get this war off the ground, you'll have to be smarter. No more flying off the handle. There's ample time for fighting. You'll get your revenge. But for now you must be patient. Do you understand?"

"Yes."

"Good."

"Did the guard say anything about the gun?" I ask him.

Jude stops walking. "Did he *see* the gun?"

I nod. "I hit him with it. That's how he got the concussion. It was our only chance out of there."

"Lord have mercy," Jude says, wiping something invisible from the corners of his mouth.

"I threatened him," I confess. "I told him if he breathed a word, I would come for him."

Jude's eyes search me. "You're a feisty one, aren't you?" He chuckles. "Your father chose well."

"*Chose?*" I say.

"The guard is a pathetically fearful man—not much of a spine in that one. If he hasn't mentioned it by now, he probably won't. He's probably faking the amnesia, which is a smart move on his part."

"He knew I wasn't bluffing. He'll be happy never to see my face again."

"I think you're right about that, but I'll keep an eye on him nonetheless." Jude spits and says, "Now listen. This is important. Does Maria know about the gun?"

"Yes."

"OK," he says softly, the wheels in his head spinning fast. "I'll talk with her about it. Not everyone is on board with our method. This group…" Jude waves his hand at the men in front of us. "These men are a mixed bag. Some aren't convinced yet about the war."

"Why not?"

"They believe there's another way to freedom."

"Maria mentioned this ridiculous notion. She isn't too keen on the idea herself."

Jude rolls his eyes. "Tell me about it. Just keep the gun to yourself, OK? Mention it to no one else."

"Fine. What's this supposed other way?"

"It's the Teacher," Jude says dismissively. "He puts all these ideas in everyone's heads. Has them thinking all sorts of things, getting people confused about the war."

"But he's a Southerner?"

"Yes, and he wants freedom for his people, but he goes about it in the strangest ways. Some days I'm convinced he'll lead the battle charge himself. Other times I feel he detests the very notion of war. It's a mess, and it's incredibly distracting." Jude spits again. "Whatever. What's important is that you're here now. The men are buzzing to meet you."

"The men? I thought I just met them."

Jude shakes his head. "You met the students. Now it's time to meet the men." He arches an eyebrow. "Or…I should say, *your* men."

We find the group lounging near a small lake, passing a bottle of wine and a basket of rye bread. My stomach rumbles at the sight of food, reminding me I haven't eaten since long before sunrise.

Maria is on the ground next to Miles, and she waves me over when she sees me. The brothers take notice, and I swell with pride.

*Yes, you may have known her longer, but I'm the one she just kissed. I'm the one she wants at her side.* An elementary level of pride consumes me. *She wants me. Which means she doesn't want you.*

Jude says, "Wait. We need to discuss the money."

"What about it?"

"Your little stunt will make a large transfer significantly more challenging. You're a marked man—no more flying under the radar."

"Tell me something I don't know. I'm beginning to think I was marked long before I arrived in the South."

"Not like this. I'll be shocked if there's not an audit requested on you in the morning. The red flags are everywhere."

"But it's *my* money," I say. "I can do with it what I want."

Jude laughs as one of the men passes him the wine. He tips the bottle to his lips and says, "And King Charles has me over for tea on Sundays." He takes a long pull on the bottle and passes it to me. I take a sip and pass the bottle to the guy standing closest, a tall man with tree-trunk arms and curly blond hair. He snatches the bottle and drains the rest of it, drawing groans from the others. The curly-haired man laughs and promises to find more. He promptly hops up to make good on the offer.

"What's his story?" I ask Jude.

Through a yawn he says, "They call him 'Petra.'"

"*Rock?*"

Jude nods. "A nickname the Teacher gave him. The guy's a real beating... but he's on our side, which is good. Petra's the kind of man who can make life difficult when you don't see eye to eye with him. But as long as he's with us, he'll do more than carry his weight. He's as fearless as they come, a natural-born leader."

"We'll need men like that." I lower my voice and add, "So what do we do about the money?"

"I'm not sure, but whatever we do must happen sooner than later. We can't sit on this. If we wait too long, the money will be gone."

"Come on. The Kingdom can't just steal my money."

"How'd that work out for your parents?"

Jude's words hit me like a shot to the gut.

"I'm sorry," he says, exasperated. "But they took your parents, OK? They can do whatever they want, Deacon. You need to get that through your skull. These people don't mess around. *They make people disappear.* Money is a total no-brainer for them."

I think for a long moment before saying, "I'll come back to the bank tomorrow and withdraw all of it. There's got to be somewhere else we can stash it."

"Out of the question. You can never step foot in the bank again. Those guards may not be members of the Centurion Guard, but that doesn't make them teddy bears. You got the jump on them once. It won't happen again."

"Then how can I get the money if I can't go to the bank?"

"By proxy," Jude says. "You can authorize someone else to access your account."

"How would I do that?"

"Not easily. You'll have to return to the Office of Record and make the request with your supervisor."

"That's out of the question."

"Why?"

"Because my supervisor is a psycho."

"You can't be serious."

"As a heart attack. She nearly choked me to death."

A few of the students have noticed our conference and are now craning their heads to get a better look at us.

"Calm down," Jude says. "None of this will be easy, but you'll have to keep your emotions in check. Otherwise you're already dead."

"Fine," I say. "But don't be surprised if I don't make it out of that building."

"I have faith in you."

Maria calls out to me. "Deacon! Stop acting so serious, and come sit with me."

"Go tomorrow," Jude orders. "First thing in the morning, and tell her to add my name to the account."

"You? But won't that be suspicious? I was thinking Maria ought to be the one."

"No. It has to be me. Maria won't understand. And I'm not sure I trust her."

"You can trust Maria," I say defensively. "If there's one thing I know, it's that she can be trusted."

Jude glares at Maria then me. "Not the time to go falling in love, kid."

"That's not your concern."

"In the morning…" Jude says, eyeing Maria. Then he looks at me. "…make the request. My last name is Iscariot. I'll secure the funds, and we'll rally the men and make the necessary procurements."

"When can I meet them?"

"Tomorrow night."

"How many are there?"

Jude smiles. "Many. I'll let the precise number be a surprise, but rest assured that we have enough to make a serious assault."

The mere thought of this enthralls me—Southerners willing and armed to do battle with the Kingdom. "I can't wait to join their ranks," I say. "I just hope I'm ready to play my role—whatever it may be."

Jude issues an anxious breath of air. "You'll play your role; trust me. Now go to her." He flicks his chin toward Maria. "While you still can."

# CHAPTER 11

I settle down next to Maria and replay the conversation with Jude in my head. The man knows more than he's letting on, but he's guided me well so far, which leads me to believe he can be trusted. After all, my father trusted him.

My father's wealth remains the most unfathomable of mysteries to me. Where did this money come from? He and my mother barely had enough to send me away to school. It doesn't make sense.

But Jude is the one with the answers.

The bread comes around, and Maria and I both take large slices that have been soaked in almond butter. I inhale the first slice and immediately ask Miles for another. He hands the basket to me and says, "Be careful with that one."

"Who? Jude?"

"He's a hawk," Miles says, his trademark smile gone.

Through a mouthful of bread, I say, "Aren't we all?"

"Yes, but we can also be diplomatic. There are many paths for the revolution. We can't rush anything."

"He's not," I say. "As far as I can tell, he's the only one with a plan—at least one he's willing to share."

"Just be careful. Keep your mind open. He isn't the only voice worth listening to."

I shove another piece of bread in my mouth and say, "I'll listen to anyone, as long as they're willing to fight."

Maria pokes her head between us. "No more scheming today," she says. "It's all so exhausting. The sun is down, and it is time for peace. So...let us have peace."

Miles laughs in agreement. "Yes...and look! Petra has found the Teacher."

"And more wine!" Maria says.

I look up to find two men walking slowly toward us. The curly-haired Petra marches proudly, holding gigantic bottles of red wine in each hand. He raises them like trophies above his head, and the group cheers in reply. More wine!

Beside Petra is a slightly built man with dark skin and short-cropped black hair. He's dressed simply, in dark trousers and a black T-shirt. Petra walks with such exuberance that the smaller man is practically absorbed into his energy. If I weren't intentionally looking for the Teacher, I don't think I would have noticed him at all. As they approach I regard the Teacher further and discover his face to be completely unremarkable. He's neither handsome nor unattractive. For a man of such fame, I expected more.

"Where has he been?" I ask Miles.

"He left early this morning, before the sunrise. He went to a quiet place for prayer."

"He does that often," Maria adds. "He wanders into the desert alone to find his energy, to pray for guidance."

Miles nods. "He *needs* the time to himself. He gets mobbed wherever he goes. It never ends."

"I don't understand how a man can get so famous," I say. "He's not even ordained in the True Religion, is he?"

Maria shakes her head. "No, he's never sought academic or religious credentials. But he doesn't need them."

"That's ridiculous. Why not?"

"Because," Miles says, "he *is* religion." He shakes his head. "There's simply no other way to describe him. He is, simply, the way."

"Yes," Maria says. "That's it exactly. He is the way—*our way home.*"

I don't understand how any person can *be* religion, so I decide to drop it. "Whatever you two say." I reach for another piece of bread. I could eat all night.

Petra arrives and says, "Look who I found wandering the streets alone!" He gives the Teacher a rowdy shove and tousles his short, messy hair. The Teacher gives it right back to him, stealing a bottle of wine and tossing it to one of the students on the ground. "I told him," Petra continues, "that everyone's been looking for him! And you know what this guy says?"

The Teacher grins and says, "Then let's leave."

The group roars with laughter.

"I'm serious!" the Teacher says, laughing at his own joke. "It's time to move on. We have work elsewhere."

"Where?" Petra asks.

"Neighboring towns," the Teacher says. "I must proclaim the message there as well. It's why I came."

Miles asks, "When do we leave?"

The Teacher looks our direction; his eyes fall on me. "Who's our guest?"

"This is Deacon," Maria says happily.

I stand and discover the Teacher is even smaller than I realized. I tower over the man. I offer him my hand, and he takes it. "It's an honor to meet you," I tell him. "I've heard much about you."

"Don't trust a word of it," he says.

"Oh, yeah?"

"Yeah. I mean, look at this crew. Have you ever seen a more awkward group of misfits in your life?"

I laugh. "Well…now that I've met their leader, it all makes sense."

Miles chokes on a piece of bread.

But the Teacher laughs. "Deacon, right?"

"That's right."

"Welcome, my friend. What brings you to this place? You look far too refined to have been in the South for long."

Maria says, "That's actually what we need to discuss with you, Teacher. Perhaps Deacon and I can speak to you in private?"

"Of course." He reaches for some wine. "But Deacon should know, straight away, that there's no need for secrets. We're all one in this place; one concern is all concern. No burden is borne in isolation."

"That's very kind of you," I say. "I couldn't agree more. It'll take all of us sacrificing to achieve freedom. We must put the good of the country before personal ambition."

"Yes," the Teacher agrees. "There will be no drum majors in this war, only servants."

Thus far the Teacher isn't what I imagined him to be. From what Maria said, I pictured a weak-bodied intellectual who didn't understand what this fight would demand. But I sense a fierce spirit in this man. He may be small physically, but his eyes burn with the passion of a warrior.

"I'm in trouble," I say. "Maria too."

"Aren't we all?" The Teacher motions to the group. "Everyone here has left the safety of home to follow this path."

"I struck a bank guard," I say. "I broke his nose badly."

"Yeah, you did!" Petra cheers, nodding his approval.

The men laugh but not the Teacher, who says, "Go on."

"It's all been taken care of," Jude interrupts. "I smoothed things over at the bank. There's no warrant for Deacon's arrest, and I highly doubt the Kingdom is searching for Maria. She's of no real consequence."

"Thanks, Jude," Maria says.

"You know what I mean," Jude says.

"But still," the Teacher says, "we can't be too careful. The Centurion Guard doesn't need much of an excuse to take us all away."

"That's right," Miles interjects. "There's already a rumor the Baptist's days are numbered. The Kingdom is growing impatient with anyone who speaks against its rule."

"Who's the Baptist?" I ask.

"My mentor," the Teacher says. "He's my closest friend and confidante—a great man."

"I look forward to meeting him."

"You won't."

"Why not?"

"He's in prison," the Teacher says. A hush falls across the group. "You must be peaceful, Deacon. Violence is not the answer right now."

"That's what I've been trying to tell him," Jude tells the Teacher. "But this kid's got a thick head." The Teacher nods at Jude.

"Violence isn't the answer?" I say. "You mean, like, for the moment?"

The Teacher takes a long look at me before speaking. "What do you hope to accomplish by way of the sword?"

I huff. "Well, first off I don't plan on using a sword. I prefer to bring guns to a firefight."

The Teacher turns away from me and addresses the group. "All of you! What do you see happening if you go to war against the Kingdom? What would success look like? Tell me. I want to know."

Petra rises to his feet. "With them dead. With our people liberated. With the Centurion Guard driven out of our land!" He makes a fist and strikes his own breast. "With victory!"

Petra's answer is met with impassioned "hurrays." Others hiss their dissent.

"Each of you must decide his or her own way," the Teacher says. "All I ask is that you consider the consequences of your actions. Ask yourself what you expect from challenging the military might of the Kingdom. Be reasonable and measure the weight of its cost."

"The weight will be heavy," I tell him. "No doubt about that. But it's worth it. Freedom is worth any price."

The Teacher furrows his dark eyebrows. "Is it?"

"Yes!" I say.

"And what will you do, Deacon, with your invaluable freedom?"

I start to tell him I won't be around to enjoy my freedom, that I have no illusions of still breathing when this war is over. But with Maria standing at my side, I can't bring myself to utter such depressing truths. "Nothing special," I say. "Just…to live in peace." I reach for Maria's hand and squeeze it tightly. My palms are laden with sweat.

The Teacher says, "I've dedicated what's left of my life to a single mission, Deacon."

"Me too."

"The time is fulfilled," he says slowly, "and the kingdom of God has come near. Repent, and believe in the good news."

"Teacher?" Petra interrupts. "There's a man here to see you."

# CHAPTER 12

The Teacher turns away from me and moves toward Petra, who gives a wide berth to the man asking for the Teacher. The stranger wears an oversize robe that covers his body from head to toe. There's a veil across his face. Not an inch of his skin is exposed to the air. The only signs of humanity are his eyes, and they're horribly bloodshot.

"So," I say to Maria, "I've met the famous Teacher."

She grins. "Isn't he wonderful?"

"If you say so."

"Give him time," Miles says. "I wasn't an immediate convert either. He's enigmatic, to put it mildly. Give him a chance."

"He speaks of God's kingdom," I say. "What does he mean by that?"

"The boys argue a lot about it," Maria says. "Some think he's speaking of the afterlife."

"And the others?"

"It's his vision," Miles says, "of what could be *now*, of what life might look like if we choose this other way to live."

"Which nobody actually understands," I say. Miles and Maria share a look, wordlessly communicating a message to which I'm not privy. "I'm right, aren't I? None of you gets it, but you're pretending because you *want* to understand."

"Like I said," Miles says gently, "it takes time."

"Well, time is what I most definitely don't have."

Petra's voice breaks urgently into our conversation. "Teacher! No! You mustn't! It's not safe."

We drop our bread and rush to find the Teacher pulling the hood off the stranger. His face is grotesque. It's covered in sores; puss oozes from his eyes, nose, and ears. Open wounds litter his skin, the pockmarks stinking so badly that we have no choice but to pinch our noses. One of the men vomits. I nearly do the same. I've never seen anything so disgusting. The man looks ancient, as if he were exhumed from a thousand-year-old grave and brought back to pungent life.

"What is that?" I say, turning away, unable to look any longer.

"*That* is a man, Deacon," Maria says. "*That* is a human being."

I turn around slowly, the putrid odor wafting over me like a plague. It takes all of my composure to remain standing, to keep my focus on the baffling scene playing out before me.

"What's wrong with him?" I ask.

"He's a leper," Miles says.

Of course I, of all people, should have recognized it. Eradicated years ago, the disease returned to the South when foreigners came to this region from the Far East.

"What's he doing here? Lepers aren't permitted within city limits. He could infect us all. There are no medications left in the South to treat leprosy. He needs to be in a colony; he needs to be isolated."

Maria ignores my concern and moves closer to the Teacher, who has now taken the man's deformed face into his bare hands. He's saying something but speaks too softly for anyone but the leper to hear. Against my better judgment, I draw closer, eager to know what's happening. I know I shouldn't do this, but I can't stop myself from following Maria. I can't believe the Teacher is *touching* a leper. It's insane.

The other men's faces are splattered with fear, and they're inching away from the Teacher and the leper. Only Maria and I move closer. I glance back at Jude, who shakes his head in dissent.

But I can't stop.

Maria was wrong. The leper's face isn't human. He looks like a monster from my worst nightmares. His eyes are sunken into his head, and his nose is unrecognizable—twisted and collapsed. I can't see his nostrils.

The leper falls to his knees, and the Teacher slows his fall as the man's legs fold in unnatural directions beneath his body. They're little more than a mangled mess of gangly, rotting flesh.

"It's not just his skin that's ravaged," Maria informs me. "The disease has destroyed his muscles too."

"This man has the most severe form of leprosy," I tell her. "That's why there are bumps on his face. The disease is advanced. He doesn't have long to live."

Maria looks askance at me. "How do you know that?"

"I studied medicine in the West."

"Are you a doctor?"

"Supposed to be."

Maria slips her arm around my waist. "What happened?"

"I came home."

"If you choose," the leper says hoarsely to the Teacher, "you can make me clean."

The Teacher squats on the ground, his face inches from the leper's wounds. Then he does the unthinkable; he kisses the man softly on the forehead, his left cheek, and once more on his right cheek. "I do choose," he says, weeping in the arms of the dying man. The Teacher then whispers into the leper's deformed ear, "Be made clean."

I look sideways at Maria. "How can he say that? He shouldn't promise such things. There's no cure for this man, not here in the South."

The Teacher stands without offering his hand to the leper. Instead he orders the man to stand. The leper obeys, springing from the ground with strength he didn't possess minutes ago. His eyes, which were bloodshot, are now clear as the morning sky. Even the leper's skin has begun to change from an ashy white to a healthy rose. Most notably, however, is the absence of the man's odor. I once again smell the magnolia blossoms of the park. The leper's face is still scarred, but puss no longer oozes from it.

"What the…?"

"Now," the Teacher says sternly, "tell no one what I have done, but go and show yourself to the religious authorities and offer your cleansing as a testimony to them."

"No," he says, his eyes bright as a child playing at the beach. "I shall tell the world of what you've done to me."

"I'm serious," the Teacher says, a power stroking through his voice. "*You will say nothing.*"

The leper turns sharply away from the Teacher and darts into the dark woods of the park, running at a blindingly fast speed.

"That man," I say. "He could barely walk. How did...?"

"Enigmatic," Miles repeats from behind me. "The Teacher is...mysterious."

We spend the rest of the evening in quiet conversation, with no further discussion of war or serious matters. The leper's visit has transformed the mood, leaving us to soberly reflect on what we've seen. I still can't believe what my eyes are trying to convince my brain it witnessed.

*That man couldn't have been healed by simple touch...could he?*

*Of course not.*

The human body is incapable of that sort of response. I'm not a doctor, but I know enough about physiology to realize that unexplainable healings don't occur within a matter of seconds. These things take time; healing is a process, not a one-off event.

Yet I can't deny the transformation I saw. The way that sickly man ran away—well, it's inexplicable. He sprinted into the distance with the prowess of an athletic champion. I don't know what to make of it except the joy I saw in the leper's eyes. That—I know—was real.

The Teacher and I don't speak with each other again this evening. He spends his time moving among the others, laughing and telling stories of past adventures. Later Maria strums an old guitar with a missing string, leading us in the songs of our ancestors. I know these lyrics by heart but am too enamored with Maria's singing voice to join the chorus. She's a throaty tenor, and her singing is the most sensual sound I've ever heard.

Her voice has the quality of an artist who sings from the most righteously truthful place of the human soul—that spot where falsehood can't exist. That place most of us are too scared to touch, much less sing from. But there she is, doing it as if it were the most natural thing in the world.

I envy that sort of honesty. Sometimes I fear there isn't an honest bone left in my body. And that worries me, rattles me deep within my spirit.

These men and Maria have been together so long that they exhibit the dynamics of a close-knit family. Their conversation follows an easy, natural, familial flow, with silence feeling as cozy as laughter. They've seen much to-gether, and while they may lack sophistication, they more than make up for it in unity. These are folks willing to go through the fire together. They're one, just as the Teacher said. Yet I wonder whether their cohesion will be able to stand the test of war. This group is kind, but I doubt their toughness and am deeply suspect of their resolve.

Eventually Maria and I break away from the reverie and find a comfortable spot in the grass, where we lie down and recount the day's events. Somehow she finds the humor in it all. She laughs loudly, imitating my horrified expression when she found me in the street.

"You were terrified!" she howls.

"That's because I thought I was going to die," I say, in stitches.

Maria laughs harder. "Well...you were!"

My laughter turns to crying. "I don't know why I'm laughing," I say, wiping away tears. "This isn't funny. They were going to kill us!"

Maria rolls onto her stomach. "You're exhausted." She sighs and throws back her gorgeous black head of hair. "We both are. It's called delirium. How are your hands and head?"

"Fine. Just scratches. Can you imagine the kind of pain that leper was in?"

"Yes," Maria says soberly. "I could see it in his eyes." She pauses to remem-ber something secret. "But physical pain is the easy part for a man like that."

"How so?"

"Physical pain can be dealt with, tolerated, and managed...but not the pain of rejection, of loneliness. That man was pushed outside the gates of society and told he was worth nothing." Maria bites her bottom lip. "I know that kind of pain, and it's inescapable."

"I hadn't thought of it that way."

She twirls a finger through my hair. "Will you do something for me?"

"Anything."

"Get rid of that gun. Throw it in the lake or something."

I shake my head. "I can't do that."

"You just said you'd do anything for me."

"No," I say, trying to smooth the tension out of my voice. "Not that."

She inches her body closer to mine. "Why not?"

I swallow hard, my heart thumping in my chest. "Because…my father gave it to me."

Maria's face tightens. "Does your father know what sort of danger that gun put you in today? It nearly got you killed," she huffs. "He should be ashamed of himself—giving you such a wretched gift."

I inch away from her and sit up in the grass. "I know you saved my life today, and I'll never be able to repay you for that, but that gun helped. You can't deny it."

Maria opens her mouth then snaps it shut. "Yes," she admits, "but it's just that I…you're right. It's just that I *hate* guns."

"It's not like I'm obsessed with them," I say. "I've never even fired one. How embarrassing is that? They're just tools—necessary tools during times like these."

Maria doesn't say anything. She just stares off into the distance, her mind quietly at work on something.

The park is now dark, with the only light coming from white holiday lights haphazardly strung through random tree branches. It's difficult to see beyond the small patch of grass where we lie, which is how I like it. It's just me and Maria, and nothing else.

I reach out my hand and stroke her hair. "Let's talk about something else. You may hate guns, but I hate arguing with you even more."

"What would you like to talk about it?" she says somewhat absently.

"Doesn't matter, as long as it's you I'm talking to. How about this park? Do you sleep here every night?"

Maria's eyes return to mine, and she relaxes into a soft smile. "No. What kind of girl do you take me for? I'm not the Baptist. I can handle only a few nights a week in this park, beautiful as it is. After that I demand a shower and a warm bed with crisp sheets."

"You have a house?"

"I stay with Petra's mother-in-law. I don't have a place of my own."

"*Petra?*"

I'm shocked at the revelation that he's married. The man seems too large, too utterly filled with vigor to be capable of such a domestically mundane relationship. I can't even picture him having a mother of his own, much less a mother-in-law. Childhood doesn't fit a guy like Petra. I imagine him walking and talking within hours of his birth, a man-baby.

"Yes, she owns a small house nearby. She lends me a bed whenever I need it. The rest of the brothers board with friends around town, whoever has a room. But Petra's mother-in-law never gives away my room."

"That's kind of her."

"Yes, well, the Teacher saved her life. She's deeply grateful for what he's trying to do."

"She was ill?"

"Strong fever. She was so close to the grave that she couldn't get up from bed. But after the Teacher went to her, she regained strength. It was miraculous. She's served him, and us, ever since."

"How many people has he healed like that?"

"Nobody knows. Hundreds? Maybe thousands? There are no records. I don't even think *he* knows how many lives he's touched. He just does it and moves on to the next person, as if nothing special has happened."

Carefully I say, "Do you think he is of the one true God?"

"Yes, very much so."

"What makes you think that?"

"Besides my own healing, I've seen unexplainable things during the time I've followed him. There's no other way to interpret how they've happened."

"Like what? What have you seen?"

Maria ties her long hair into a loose bun. A single black hair falls lightly across her face. "There was an evening on a boat," she says, "out at sea. The Teacher wanted to escape the crowds, but other boats set sail and followed us. Soon after, a great windstorm arose, and the waves beat into the boat. It was quickly filling with water. I thought we would die—we all did."

"And the Teacher?"

"Asleep. He was reclining in the stern of the boat, his head on a pillow, sleeping like a child. We—somebody; I don't remember who—shook him awake. Petra asked him if he cared that we were going to drown. I remember that clearly, the fire in Petra's eyes. One of the other boats on the water had just capsized, and we heard screams over the driving rain. It was awful. I told Miles we had to do something, but he said we'd drown if we tried to save them. That's when the Teacher sat up. He looked frustrated and tired, and then he stared out into the storm for what felt like a very long time. Calmly he said, 'Peace. Be still.' Not a second later, the storm died, giving way to the deadest calm I've ever seen on the water. We were all stunned. Then the Teacher looked at us like we were the crazy ones, and said, 'Why are you afraid? Have you still no faith?'"

"What did you say?"

"Nothing. No one said a word. That was the first time I was afraid of him." Maria's eyes cut away from me. "We all were." She lets out a long sigh and lies flat against the earth. Reliving this tale has sapped her of energy. After a time she adds, "What sort of man commands the wind and the sea?"

I have no answer to that question. I lie down next to her and close my eyes, trying to imagine all those people tossing about in the rough waters, believing they were about to die. Then, a moment later, the waters were placid. Did they know it was the Teacher? Did they even care?

Maria and I say nothing for a long while, testing the waters of silence between us and discovering we float gently in their current, like two children born of the sea. We're as laidback as lifetime lovers, yet we haven't even known each other twenty-four hours. Despite the tragedies of the last few months, and even today, I've never been happier at any moment in my life. I could lie in this park with Maria until we both turn gray and sink into the soil.

Maria breaks the silence. "What did your father say to you?"

"What do you mean?"

"When he gave you the gun. What did he say?"

"Oh." I fold my hands behind my head and keep my eyes closed. "I wanted to tell you on the train. I tried to, actually." I draw in a deep breath of courage then let out the truth. "My parents were abducted by the Kingdom and sent north. A telegram arrived a few months later, telling me they were dead."

"Oh, my God! That's...no. That's...so awful."

Maria sits up sharply. I don't move. "I left school and traveled home."

"Deacon, I'm sorry. I...I didn't know."

She rests her hand on my chest, and I unlock my hands so I can touch her arm as she leans her weight against me. Her skin is as smooth as anything I've ever touched. It's like touching the skin of Eve seconds after God fashioned her from Adam's rib. *Purity.*

"I went to the bank because my father left a key to a safe-deposit box."

"*That's* how you got the money?" she says. "The money you believe will keep you off a Kingdom cross?"

"Yes, and the gun."

"But how did—?"

"Jude," I say.

"Oh."

"My father was desperate for me to have this gun."

"Who was your father?"

"That's what I'm trying to find out. He and my mother were a short step up the ladder from poverty. But then I came home and discovered a gun and a fortune."

"That's very strange."

"There's more." I hesitate and ask myself whether I really want to say the next part. I find myself talking before I can decide. "I think my father was involved in the resistance."

"Lots of people around here are."

"This is different." I open my eyes to see Maria's black eyes hovering above me. "Jude was waiting for me at the bank, as if he knew I'd be coming. And apparently so did my father. Now it feels like there's something I'm supposed to do, something important."

"You're making me nervous, Deacon."

"Me too."

"You don't have to do anything you don't want," Maria says. "I'm sure your father wouldn't want you mixed up in this. He'd probably be furious if he knew you abandoned your studies to come here."

"I'm not sure about that."

Maria grabs my shirt and pulls me up by the collar. "I need you to promise me something."

"I think we've established I can't do that, Maria."

"What if I said I'd run away with you?"

"What?"

"I know you've thought of it. I feel it in you."

"I...don't know what to say."

"Say you'll do it. We can go south, to my old country."

"You'd leave the Teacher? Abandon the way?"

"For you? I'd do anything."

I don't hesitate. "Yes. Let's do it. We can leave at first light!"

"But you must promise."

"Promise what?"

"That you'll leave the gun. I know your father gave it to you, but you won't need it if we're leaving the South."

I've arrived at the crossroads my father often spoke about. He said there comes a moment in a man's life when he must choose the direction in which he will go, and everything will hang in the balance. Some paths lead to peace, while others only despair and destruction. Some lift a man up to the heavens, and some take him down to the pit. It's all in the decision; the decision determines the destiny.

I make mine with an ease I didn't expect. I've come home for a war I won't attend. Instead I'll follow love south.

"OK," I say, pulling the gun from my waistband. "I'll throw it in the lake."

A breath of excited air escapes Maria's mouth, and she pulls me in. Our lips crash against each other in a cosmic celebration of our future, which is now as wild and free as the air of Geth Park.

# CHAPTER 13

When I'm certain Maria is asleep, I slip away to the lakeshore. Before I leave I take a moment to let my eyes linger on her cocoa skin, which seems to glow in the dark. Her full lips are parted slightly as she breathes feminine, delicate breaths. She appears to be the most fragile creature on God's earth, though I know she's far from it. I silently promise her I won't be gone long, and then I slink down to the water.

When I reach the beach, I slip off my shoes and walk into the shallow water that laps against the shore. I survey the area to ensure I'm alone then withdraw my weapon, holding it low against my side. A pang of guilt strikes as I flash to a fabricated memory of my father storing this gun at the Oxford Trust, praying I would one day come for it.

*If he saw me now, what would he think? Would he hate me for this betrayal?*

The idea that my father was enmeshed in the resistance is laughable. He was a soft-spoken, gentle man—not a conspirator. I can't imagine him speaking in whispers, hiding among shadows, and plotting to overthrow the Kingdom.

The man spent his evenings peacefully with my mother, working on his oily motorbike while she tended to her garden. They were simple, tea-drinking people who enjoyed sober days and solemn nights. Their greatest ambition in life was to see me become a physician.

Yet here I am gripping my father's illegal weapon. I simply don't understand it. I'm struck with the urge to examine the gun for some clue that will shed light on this mystery, but I know I can't. I need to sling it into the water and be done with it, before I get any crazy ideas.

I'm in love now, and that's reason enough for me to leave. But even if it weren't, the forces conspiring against me should drive me away from here. Jude is wrong; the Kingdom is hunting me. I sent a Kingdom guard to the hospital today. Jude said a report wasn't written, but if he's mistaken and my name was brought to the attention of the authorities, I can't waltz into the Office of Record and expect to walk out a free man. I'm sure Dr. Stone is already salivating at the thought of wrapping her cold hands around my neck again.

I must leave; there's no other choice to make.

Then there's Legion, the man who kills Centurion Guards with his bare hands. What would I do if he came for Maria and me? I couldn't stop him from dragging her back to that pit. And what about all those eyes in the tunnel? How many were there? Five hundred? Five thousand?

Then there's the Teacher. He probably deals in the dark arts, which explains Legion's hatred of him. But his motives, like Legion's, remain unclear. It's clear he's sensitive to our cause, but he's far from a dedicated resistance fighter. I've heard him say nothing of the war, except that it will be costly. Not much of a revolutionary.

What does he want? And why does he risk his life to heal those who are sick and troubled? What's in it for him? I find it tough to trust a man I don't understand.

It's all a moot point, because at sunrise Maria and I will be gone.

I look at the gun and allow my anger to kindle. *My father wanted me to throw away my life for his war.* As soon as the thought is hatched, it takes root like a ravenous weed, slithering around all that is good in the garden of my mind.

The Kingdom has trillions upon trillions of Worlds at its disposal. What did he think I could do with a single gun?

I'm just about to throw the gun when a voice stops me.

"Wait!" Jude screams, running toward me. "What do you think you're doing?"

I hoped to escape the park without having to face Jude's judgmental eyes. I figured if I never had to see him again, I could pretend as if our whole encounter never had happened; it would be a hazy dream I eventually could erase from my mind.

"I'm sorry," I say, "but this life isn't for me. I plan to leave at first light."

"You can't be serious," he says, out of breath.

I offer him the gun. "Take it. It's yours."

"Is this about Maria?" he says.

"No."

"Don't mistake me for a fool, Deacon."

"I don't, but there's nothing to discuss. Do you want the gun or not?"

"No, I don't want it."

"Then it's going in the water."

"I don't want the gun because it's useless in my hands."

*Just throw it,* I think. But something stops me. "What does that mean? I'm sure you can point and fire just the same as me."

"That gun isn't supposed to be fired."

"Then it's a pointless gun."

"The guard you hit doesn't think so."

"I should have shot him," I say bitterly.

Jude curses and kicks his foot in the sand. "Don't you want to know what the gun is for?"

"No."

"Can you calm down long enough to try and understand a few things?"

"I don't want to understand. I'm leaving."

"Let me get this straight—you're going to let *one day* with that woman destroy everything your father planned?"

I turn and throw the gun toward the beach. It lands with a muffled thud.

"My father was a laborer!" I scream. "Nothing more! Get that through your thick skull and leave me alone. I'm done talking."

I start to stalk off through the shallow water, but Jude grabs me. "Your father was the greatest man I've ever known! Your father organized an army of five thousand men ready to die valiantly in war. Your father was the brightest hope the South has seen since the end of the Great War." He takes a deep breath and searches the night sky. Then, in a softer voice, he says, "Your father believed his son would carry on his legacy."

"My father organized no army. You've lost your mind."

"Five thousand strong men," Jude says. "And we're not talking about some backwoods militia that's only good at running their mouths. These are legitimate soldiers, Deacon. Men with training, battle tested. Men who understand the sacrifice and are willing to pay it."

"How could my father have done that? It's like you're talking about a complete stranger."

81

"Your father protected you. He wanted your life to be a peaceful one. He was no war hawk. Your father, unlike so many would-be messiahs, understood that war is only a means to an end and not the end in itself. He accepted that his fate would lead him to violence, but he wanted something better for you. That's why he sent you out West. But even a father's dream can't circumvent the will of God."

"You're asking me to believe that my whole life—everything I've known—was a lie. Do you realize that?"

"No," Jude says solemnly. "I'm asking you to believe the one true thing about your life."

"And what's that?"

"That your father wasn't wrong."

"About what?"

"About your being the man our people have waited for, the Christ long predicted in the Scripture."

"What?"

"The anointed one, Deacon—the one sent by God to make it right."

My heart jumps erratically in my chest. Sharp pangs are followed by dangerously long gaps before another shuddering beat slams across my rib cage. It's as if air is alternately blown into then sucked out of my lungs before it's had a chance to oxygenate my blood. I feel faint, and black spots stain my vision.

Jude leaves me where I stand to find the gun in the sand. When he returns, I stand frozen in silence.

"Here," he says, offering the handle of the gun. "Read the inscription."

"What?"

"On the bottom. Read it."

I take the gun and find two numbers inscribed on the bottom of the handle: 1-12. "How did I miss this?" I say.

"Those numbers mean anything to you?"

I wait a long moment before answering. When I'm ready, I say, "My birthday."

"That's right," Jude says.

"What does this mean?"

"You were the reason your father joined the resistance. He told me he had the date inscribed before he went into battle. Your father understood that war does things to a man, and no matter how brave and prepared he might be, battle is ferocious and paralyzing. He wanted to ensure that if he ever found himself in a position where he wanted to retreat or surrender, he'd have a tangible reminder of why he was fighting. January twelfth was the most important day of his life, the day everything changed. If a man lives only for himself, he might not be willing to die. But if he lives for someone else, he'll happily lay down his life. You were his beginning, and you would be his end."

I collapse into the sand and weep. After a time—I don't know how long—Jude puts his hand on my shoulder. "Come with me," he says. "Meet the men. I'll have you back before sunrise. If you still want to leave, I won't try to stop you."

"I...don't know. If Maria—"

"She'll never know you're gone. I'll bring you back before she wakes up. I'm asking you to trust me."

I don't want to go. I want to walk back to Maria and lie down beside her in the grass. I want to watch her sleep and listen to her breaths. I want to watch her body twitch and wonder what she's dreaming about. Then, just before the sun rises, I want to wake her with a kiss and tell her it's the first day of the rest of our lives together.

"Deacon," Jude says, "come see what your future could be. You owe that much to your father. *Please.*"

"Not true," I say, standing up and shaking off the sand. "I owe him my life."

We ride fast out of town, beyond the city limits, and into the rolling countryside. Jude, who seems to know more about my life than I do, knew I could ride a motorcycle. From the lake he led me stealthily to two old Ducati dirt bikes hidden beneath a tangle of overgrown brush. He pulled the bikes out and said, "We'll have to ride fast to make it there and back before sunrise. Stay close, and don't lay it down. I don't have helmets."

I told him I'd never worn a helmet in my life.

We kept the Ducatis in idle and pushed them along with our feet like kids on bicycles first learning to ride. We stayed this way until we were out of the park and on a dirt road that ran parallel to the highway but was hidden from it by tall oaks. Then we opened the throttles.

In practically no time we're outside the city and riding hard across the rough country, the Ducati absorbing the shock beneath me in spotty, uneven bounces. Other than the beams from our headlights, the land around us is pitch black; Oxford sleeps while we ride.

An hour later we reach the coast. Jude slows down, and I follow his lead off the dirt road, through a small opening in the woods and onto a terribly pitted, two-lane concrete highway. We ride slowly for another minute, the pavement a welcome respite from the bounce of the trail, until Jude raises his hand, signaling for me to stop. "You see that bridge?" He points in the distance, and I can just make out the outline of a suspension bridge against the black of the sky. If I hadn't already been familiar with this bridge, there would be no way for me to recognize it. But I do.

"You're insane if you think I'm riding across that," I say.

"You know this bridge?"

"Of course." I shut off the bike and swing my leg off. "The Bridge of Banishment—the only way on or off the leper colony."

Jude nods.

"Well," I yawn, stretching my arms behind my back. "This has been fun, but if it's all the same to you, I think I'll pass on contracting leprosy tonight."

"The men are on the other side of that bridge, Deacon."

"You're crazy if you think I'm going to ride into that colony. There hasn't been a vaccine in the South for over twenty years. That entire island is a petri dish of disease. No way...not going."

"How do you think the army is able to meet without being discovered?" I clear my throat but don't say anything. "It's the only place the Centurion Guard doesn't regularly patrol."

"Not true."

"How's that?"

"Geth Park," I tell him. "There were no centurions there."

"Because the Kingdom trusts the religious authorities to keep an eye on people like the Teacher and his followers. They're not overly concerned by wannabe philosophers and poets." Jude shakes his head. "But us? You and I are another story. They know we're dangerous."

"And the men want to meet me?"

"Badly."

"Then have them come to me. Ride across the bridge and order them to come out."

"You're joking, right?"

"We don't have much time," I say. "I *will* be back in the park before sunrise, with or without you."

Jude flies off his bike and shoves me in the chest with unexpected speed and power. I stumble backward in the darkness and trip on myself, landing hard on the pavement with my elbows. "You listen to me, you sorry little brat!" he shouts. "I swore to your father that I'd make this meeting happen. I know you can't possibly understand what I'm about to say, but hear it anyway. That man was a father to me. He was the only person who ever cared if I lived or died. My mother abandoned me to my drunk of a father the second I left her breast. When I was eleven, it was me who went off to work because he couldn't bother to set down the bottle." Jude takes a breath. "I killed him when I was fifteen."

"You...killed your own father?"

"I preferred it to the alternative."

"I'm sorry," I say softly.

Jude snaps his fingers. "I'd have taken your father's place on that train in a heartbeat." He lifts me up by collar. "So—may the gods help me—you're going across that bridge if I have to drag you."

# CHAPTER 14

W e cross the bridge.

Thinking of Jude's mother and father reminds me of why I came home in the first place. I'm far from the only person who's suffered. The South is a country that baptizes its babies in pain; its people wear disillusionment like jewels around their necks. Most of the children here have experienced more heartache before their tenth birthday than the average adult in the West does in a lifetime.

Parents are hauled away by train to the northern camps. Children are forced into adulthood at tender ages, just as Jude was. Violence has become the currency of the market. I saw my first crucifixion on my eighth birthday. Watching nails driven through a body takes something from you that you don't get back.

We've never known freedom, and there's no one left from the generation that did. When I was a child, the last of the old folks were still living, and their stories permeated our land with a faint but very real hope. They spoke of the implicit joy of travel, of being able to pack up your family and explore the world. I heard tales of what it was like to live without the fear of the Kingdom's iron fist. People were free to do with their lives as they saw fit.

The only reason I was allowed to leave for school was my test scores. The Kingdom, through standardized testing, decides very early in people's lives who gets to continue with education and who must stop and enter the work force. My scores were very high, which meant I got to keep going. When I completed my primary schooling, my vocational testing indicated medicine would be my profession. But this was no accident. My parents had meticulously prepared me for this path since my childhood, beginning with their decision to read *Grey's Anatomy* to me when most children heard fairy tales about courageous princes and evil warlocks. The day I left on that train was the culmination of many years of planning.

I never minded. I've loved the human body for as long I can remember and want to bring healing to pain.

I lied to Dr. Stone. I haven't always been interested in medicine; I became interested the instant my parent asked me to study it. Even then I understood they were trying to save me from this place.

From the time I was old enough to walk, my parents warned me about the leper colony. Under no circumstances was I to cross the bridge I just have. When I asked my father what was on the other side, he simply told me, "Death."

Which was a good enough answer for me.

I follow Jude down an old cobblestone road that runs alongside the battered fortress that now functions as a prison for the several hundred lepers who live on this island. I lift my shirt above my face, but it does little to mask the odor of rotting, petrified flesh that permeates the air.

We ride for another few minutes before arriving at the back of a concrete amphitheater. We kill the bikes and walk silently to the outer edge of the theater, which I discover is filled with men. At least two thousand of them are standing on the concrete rows, which are lit up by torches. Their attention is fixed firmly on the stage, where two men are trying to murder each other with their fists.

One of the boxers is short and fast. The other is unreasonably tall, with a reach that's categorically unfair. Both men wear red padded helmets and matching gloves. The tall man throws a punishing jab that sends his opponent to the floor. The bloodthirsty crowd erupts with pleasure. This is what they've hoped to see.

The smaller man scrambles to his feet and bulrushes the giant, wrapping his arms around his waist. He lifts the crown of his head into the tall man's chin, and it splits wide open.

The smaller man unleashes lightning-fast punches into the giant's abdomen. The punches strike in rapid fire, one after another, but they're totally useless—as innocuous as an underwater punch. The giant then raises his left hand high and brings it down in an illegal strike against the top of the shorter man's head. The giant follows this with a devastating hook that knocks his opponent out cold. The crowd goes wild as he lifts his massive arms in victory.

I'm just about to ask Jude who this giant is when the man removes his helmet and shakes loose his blond hair. And there I see it…the face of the centurion I've dreamt about for three years. It's the giant who took my mother from the train platform.

I draw my gun and point it at Jude when he tries to stop me. Then I go after my man.

I bound down the steps like a mountain lion after its prey—graceful, fast, and deadly.

The men notice, and their cheering gives way to murmurs of questions, gasps, and accusations. I think I hear someone say, "That's him!"

When I reach the stage, the Nordic and I make eye contact, and I know instantly that he recognizes me. His bravado can't hide what I see behind his icy blue eyes: fear.

"*You!*" I say, raising the gun before me and taking dead aim at the center of his wide chest. "*You!*"

"Deacon!" Jude cries out. "Stop! Deacon!"

I rush the centurion and jab the barrel into his muscular chest. "What did you do with my mother? Tell me! Did you put them on the train yourself? Tell me before you die! Tell me before I blow your head off!"

"Deacon!" Jude pleads from behind me. "Get a hold of yourself!"

I keep the gun dug firmly into the Nordic's powerful chest. "I saw this man grab my mother. He's responsible for their deaths."

The giant centurion says, "If you know what's good for you, you'll lower that gun, boy." His voice is so deep that even though I'm the one with a gun, I'm suddenly terrified to be standing so close to him. His voice is just not human.

"Deacon," Jude says, grabbing my shoulder, "Henrik defected from the Centurion Guard. He's on our side now."

"So it was you!" I say. "Why were my parents taken north? Who gave the order? Tell me!"

Henrik nods toward Jude. "Didn't he tell you?"

"Yes," Jude says, a mixture of exasperation and anxiety in his voice. "I did. Henrik—if it even was Henrik—was just following orders, Deacon. Your parents were selected because of your father's leadership of these men." Jude waves his arms in reference to the now silent men of the amphitheater.

I ignore Jude. "I want to know what you did with my mother and father, Henrik. I'm not going to ask again." I pull the hammer back on the pistol, having already decided to kill him, no matter his answer.

A faint smile appears across Henrik's face. "I wonder," he says, "if you understand the consequences of aiming that gun at me." I move the gun from his chest and raise the barrel until it rests neatly between his blue eyes. I silently curse my shaking hand. Henrik lets out a quick, breathless laugh. "I don't think you do."

"Let me guess. Don't draw a gun unless you plan on using it. That sound right?"

Henrik nods, a smirk at the corner of his mouth. "It does."

"Deacon," Jude says, "I'm begging you."

I give Jude the tiniest moment of attention, but it's enough for Henrik, who moves much too fast for a man of his size. In one motion he grabs the barrel and turns the gun over and out of my hand, bending my wrist at a horribly unnatural angle. The pain is searing.

I jump and kick the gun out of his hand, sending it to the ground. A single errant round fires off. I don't know where the bullet lands.

I dive for the gun, sliding roughly across the concrete stage. As soon as my fingers reach it, Henrik jerks hard on my ankles, pulling me toward him like a ragdoll. I flip my body over and swing my fist hard across his jaw.

The pain is tremendous. My hands feel as if they're on fire, but I have no choice but to punch him again. It's useless, though, like punching steel. His weight atop me is crushing.

Henrik smiles wide, his mouth flooded with blood, and cries, "Again! Again!"

I scream furiously and lurch my body upward, smashing his nose with my head. Henrik recoils to cup his bloody nose. He may be large, but he isn't invincible. He's just a man, and all men fear pain.

I jump to my feet and rush the fool. I lift my boot high and bring it down sharply on the crown of his head. My hands may be useless, but my legs are more than game for this fight. I plant one foot and use the other to kick his jaw like a soccer ball. Blood spews from his mouth like a volcano spitting hot lava. I let out a fiery cry of passion and kick Henrik again. His head bounces grossly and unconsciously against the ground. I kick him again and again.

The amphitheater roars with delight.

Time slows as I raise my head and take in the bizarre, dreamlike scene. Every man in the amphitheater has risen to his feet. They're a pack of rabid dogs worked into a feeding frenzy. They holler. They pump their fists high in the air. Some embrace each other, smiling as if they've conquered the Kingdom. Many pull off their shirts and swing them insanely above their heads. Others howl like wolves at the moon.

Then the chanting starts. It takes my brain too long to understand what they're saying, but when I do, I shudder.

"Messiah," they chant. "Messiah."

Then they lift me to their shoulders.

# CHAPTER 15

J ude and I make it back to the park just after sunrise.

Once the men hoisted me in the air, time began to move very fast, and before I knew it, morning had nearly arrived. It was extremely difficult to leave the men, especially after their plan was explained to me, but I insisted we return.

Even now, knowing what I must do, I can't bear the thought of letting Maria down—of abandoning her. I desperately need to see her this morning so I can explain my intentions. I'll need her to agree with the plan, and then Jude says I can unveil the life she and I will live together once this is all over. Because it's not true, after all, that my fate is sealed. I don't have to die to see my people freed. Some of us will die—that much is certain—but others of us are destined for roles so great that our deaths must be postponed.

I'm one such person. I see that now. It's what my father wanted.

The plan is ingenious, but it'll take a great deal of work—work I'm ready and able to do. I'm still unsure whether I'm "the One" our people have waited for, but the men are certain of it. Still it's a strange thing to think about oneself—that I'm the hope of an entire people, the One that God sent to make things right. The One prophesied about in the Scripture. Yet I can't deny the puzzle pieces are fitting together.

Jude and I hide the bikes in the brush and make our way back to where the Teacher and the others were sleeping near the lake. But when we arrive, they're gone.

"Where did they go?" I say.

"Relax," Jude says. "The Teacher often starts very early, rising with the sun. He's probably just trying to escape the crowds. He never stays in one place for long, which, as you've probably surmised, will be a challenge for our plan. The Teacher's schedule is unpredictable."

"I need to find Maria *now*," I say.

"Easy." Jude yawns and lies down in the grass. "You need to sleep. Rest now, and we'll catch up with the others this afternoon."

"You can sleep, but I'm going to find them."

"Suit yourself," Jude says, closing his eyes. "They're probably on the other side of the lake."

It takes me an hour to find them, but I finally do. It turns out the Teacher is more famous than I realized, which makes it relatively easy to locate him. I hitched a ride with some fishermen across the lake; they told me the Teacher had crossed it earlier with his students. I gave them each a hundred Worlds, and they fed me a breakfast of fish and black coffee.

Once I'm on the other side, they're easy to find. Judging by the size of the crowd, one would think King Charles himself had come to Oxford. I snake my way through the thick drove until I can see and hear the Teacher.

A boy in dirty clothes stands next to me. I ask him, "What is he teaching today?"

The boy, in an excited voice, says, "He's just appointed twelve men to whom he has granted authority. They too will cast out demons and proclaim the message."

"What do you make of this man, the one they call the Teacher?"

"Some say he's gone out of his mind," the boy says. "The religious authorities—those men down there." He points to a group of serious-looking men garbed in the flowing robes of the religious authorities. "They just shouted that the Teacher is Beelzebub, and as the ruler of the demons, he casts out demons."

"And what do you—"

"Shh!" the boy says, putting a finger to his lips. "I'm trying to listen!"

"How can Satan cast out Satan?" the Teacher says loudly, looking directly at the angry-looking religious authorities. "If a kingdom is divided against itself, that kingdom cannot stand. And if a house is divided against itself, that house will not be able to stand. And if Satan has risen up against himself and is divided, he cannot stand, but his end has come." The Teacher moves his gaze with pointed precision, somehow finding my eyes among all these people. Then he says to me and only me, "But no one can enter a strong man's house and plunder his property without first tying up the strong man; then indeed the house can be plundered."

The boy turns to me and, with a tremble in his voice, says, "I think he's talking to—"

"Me," I say, a fresh wave of terror washing over me. "He's talking to me."

I want to run, but fear paralyzes me. Last night I faced a giant without an ounce of dread, but one glare from the Teacher and I become tepid as a child.

Fortunately the Teacher spares me any further attention and carries on with his teaching, directing his message toward the larger gathering of people. I search the crowd for Maria but don't find her. After a time the Teacher is interrupted when someone from the crowd says, "Your mother and your brothers and sisters have been asking for you."

"And who are my mother and my brothers?" The Teacher looks at those seated nearest to him. "Here are my mother and my brothers! Whoever does the will of God is my brother and sister and mother." The crowd cheers with delight, and I can't help compare the uproar with the cries of the men I heard the night before. Their cry was for battle. The harder I kicked the Nordic giant, the louder those men roared. But the people of the park cheer for family and unity. Their voices are a sweet, if not naïve, offertory to the one true God.

It enrages me. How can the Teacher deny his family, the very fabric of his being? What I wouldn't give to have one second with my mother and father. And here the Teacher brushes his family off as if they're expendable shreds of garbage. I'm on the verge of voicing my anger when I find Maria.

She's seated on the ground not far from the Teacher. She looks my way as soon as my eyes fall upon her. Her black eyes glisten when she sees me, and her smile brightens the already blue-and-gold sky. She's radiant in the morning sun. We stare at each other for a long while as the Teacher speaks, but I don't hear a word of what he says.

I have no idea how long this goes on before the screams of children bring me back to reality. The screaming grows louder as people scatter, gathering children in their arms and running in every direction.

Black clouds appear from nowhere, and a lightning bolt flashes across the sky before a roll of thunder shakes the earth. "What's happening?" I say to the boy who stands bravely next to me. "What is it? What's going on?"

He points to a figure moving in the distance. "There," he says. "The monster from the tombs."

"Who?"

"I don't know his name, only that he used to live among the tombs in the country of the Gerasenes and that he couldn't be restrained. Chains and shackles do nothing to him. He breaks them all. I'm told he can't be killed."

"All men can be killed," I say.

"That's the problem, sir. He's not a man."

"Then what is he?"

"I told you...a monster."

"I don't believe in monsters."

"You will soon."

# CHAPTER 16

The boy is right.

I know because I've already met this monster.

I move against the tide of people and call out to Maria, but she can't hear me over the commotion. I see Miles take her by the arm, and they vanish into the crowd. I keep moving, shoving people where I have to, until I see the Teacher emerge from the sea of people.

He's walking out to meet Legion.

I run after him.

Legion bows before the Teacher and, in his awful hiss of a voice, spits out, "What have you to do with me, Teacher, son of the most high God? I adjure you by God, do not torment me."

As if meeting a new friend, the Teacher says, "What is your name?"

"My name is Legion! For we are many!"

"Teacher!" I say, running up behind him. "Teacher, it's me, Deacon." The Teacher and Legion pay me a quick glance before directing their attention back to each other. "Teacher, I..."

The Teacher waves his hand in the air, and my tongue freezes; I literally can't speak. It feels like my tongue has ballooned to the size of my hand.

"Please!" Legion screams, his voice sounding entirely different now, like that of a hoarse old man. Then it changes again, this time sounding like the squeal of a tiny girl. It happens again, then again, until a multitude of voices simultaneously explode out of him. They scream, "Don't send us away! We can't go back! We can't go back! We can't go back! Keep us here!" The cacophony of voices is the shrillest sound I've ever heard. I put my hands to my ears to mute the noise, but it's pointless. "Send us into the swine!" they howl. "Let us enter them. Give us the swine to torment!"

The Teacher says, "Come out of the man, you unclean spirits!"

At these words Legion falls limply to the ground, as if he's suffered a massive heart attack. He doesn't move. An invisible cloud of sound travels away from his body and near the lake, where young men are herding pigs. The pigs squeal horribly before stampeding away. They run off a small cliff and fall into the lake below.

Then there's silence.

One of the few townsmen who stayed behind to witness this event, points at the Teacher and says, "You, Teacher, must leave this place. You…are not welcome here. Take your students and leave. Please."

Other people, seeing that Legion has become calm, flood back into the area, echoing what this man has just said. The entire crowd, which moments before had been captivated by the Teacher, now demands his departure. They want no part of whatever power tamed Legion and killed those pigs.

The Teacher ignores their requests and moves closer to Legion, just as he did with the leper, showing no fear.

"Teacher," I say slowly, my tongue returning to its normal size. "I know this man. He's your enemy and can't be trusted."

"Maria told me what he did to you," the Teacher says. "Are you afraid of him?"

"He…has immense power, but no, I fear no man."

The Teacher laughs softly. "Suit yourself." He pats Legion's cheek as if comforting a child and asks me, "This man threatened your life?"

"He tried to," I say.

"And if he came for you? What would you do?"

"Fight him," I say defiantly. "Kill him."

The Teacher lifts his eyes, and I see a new kind of sadness in them. He notices me favoring my swollen wrist, which I've wrapped tightly with a bandage the fishermen gave me. "You seem to have an affinity for violence."

"Not violence," I say. "Justice."

"You're no match for Legion," the Teacher says bluntly.

"Maybe not before." I motion to his limp body lying on the ground.

The Teacher helps Legion to his feet. His legs shake beneath him, and I'm surprised to see there is light in his eyes and a red flush to his skin. He's a handsome, ruddy man, which makes me angry. "Teacher," Legion says, "please…take me with you. Let me be your student. Let me follow your way."

The Teacher smiles proudly at him, happy with the job he's done. "You may follow the way but in your own time. Go home and rest for now. You've been through a great ordeal, and the time has come for your family and friends to care for you. Go home and tell them how much the Lord has done for you and what mercy he has shown you."

"But Teacher, I have no family in this country. You mustn't…please take me with you. I have no one."

Legion weeps and falls to his knees. I'm embarrassed for him.

"You have my decision," the Teacher says. "Following now would be too strenuous for you; trust me. There's great trouble ahead. Now go and take your leave. There are good and righteous people in this town who'll provide for you."

If I didn't hate Legion so much, I might feel sorry him. The entire city thinks he's mad, and now he has nowhere to turn and no one to love him. The Teacher clearly doesn't know what he's talking about. Everyone in Oxford is terrified of Legion; there isn't a soul within a hundred miles who'll take him into their home. But that's not my problem. The best news is that he's lost control of his dark powers.

Which means I could kill him if I wanted to.

And I do.

The Teacher leaves us and returns to where his remaining students are seated. I kneel and whisper into Legion's ear, "Hey, old friend." I slap his cheek, just as the Teacher did, and run my hand through his greasy hair. Then I pull on it sharply, tearing a clump of hair loose from the roots. Legion flinches, and I grab another chunk and yank harder. "You nearly killed me," I say.

"Please," Legions whispers, tears streaming down his exhausted, filthy face. "I'm a broken man."

"You have no idea what 'broken' is," I say. "But I look forward to showing you." I release my grip, but a few matted hairs stick to my fingers. "I'm taking Maria away from this place. We're going to start a new life together, a world away from you. I'm going to give her the life she deserves, the one you robbed her of, you sorry sack of—"

"Deacon!"

I turn sharply to see Maria glaring down at me, holding a hand over her mouth.

I stand up. "Maria, I'm sorry I was gone this morning, but I can explain everything to you. I have great news."

She rushes toward me. "I thought maybe yesterday was a dream." Her black eyes glimmer. "You were here one second and gone the next."

"Never," I say. "I'm never leaving you. I have to go back to the Office of Record this morning, but after I explain why—"

She shakes her head furiously. "No. It's not safe there, especially for you. You can't go there. You'll be arrested. You'll never make it out of that building."

"Trust me," I say. "I know what I'm doing, but I need you to stay close to Miles and the Teacher while I'm gone. Things are going to heat up in the next days, but after that…" I pull Maria's face close to mine and whisper, "We'll go south. Just the two of us, OK?"

"Deacon—"

"Shh," I say, kissing her forehead. "If you can trust me, we'll have everything we've ever wanted."

"Deacon…" Maria places her hands on my chest.

"What is it?"

She takes a deep breath, and I know something is terribly wrong.

"I'm leaving the Teacher."

"I don't understand," I say.

She nods tenderly toward Legion. "He has no one."

"Which is who he deserves…*no one*."

"No one…but me. "

"You're the last person on earth he deserves! Was this even your idea? No…it was the Teacher's, wasn't it?"

The Teacher is off in the distance, lecturing to another eager but smaller crowd.

I shout to him, "Was this your idea?" He gives me a brief look of dismissal before returning his attention to his rapt audience. "Did the Teacher put you up to this?" I ask Maria.

"What sort of woman would I be if I left him? He'll die, Deacon."

Legion, who's still kneeling at my feet, begins to stand up. I plant my boot on his hand and dig down until I hear bones crunch. "Who cares?" I say. "Have you forgotten that he tried to kill me yesterday? As in, like, less than twenty-four hours ago? And now you want to…what? Forget our plans so you can nurse him back to health? Let him die!"

Maria begins to cry. "Deacon…you're so angry. I wish you'd harness your passion for something bigger."

I curse and spit on the ground. "You're the best thing that ever happened to me, Maria. Don't leave me. I'm begging you."

Maria cries harder. Everything in me tells me to apologize and take her in my arms. Just like when I saw her in the Office of Record, all I want to do is make it better. Yet I don't embrace her. Instead I stand still, like a centurion at attention, and watch her suffer.

Finally she says, "The Teacher says the whole law and all the prophets can be summed up in a single commandment."

"I wish the Teacher would do less talking and more doing."

"Love others as you love yourself," she says. "That's what he teaches the people. Did you know that?"

"It's impossible to love another person as much as yourself," I say. "It can't be done."

"Maybe not," Maria admits, dabbing at the corners of her eyes. "But we can try, can't we?"

"What about me?" I say, taking her by the shoulders and drawing her close. "Don't I deserve your love? What makes Legion so damn important?"

"This man was my husband." She lowers her voice. "We shared a bed." I dig my heel harder into Legion's hand, and he moans. "I know he's done terrible things," Maria says, "but I also know that if it weren't for the Teacher's generosity, I wouldn't have made it. I can't live with myself unless I do the same for Alejandro. We must extend mercy."

The way she says his name, with tenderness, tells me there's no convincing her otherwise. And deep within me—somewhere—I know she's right. But I won't admit it to her. I can't.

"And yes," Maria says, "you deserve my love more than anyone. And I'll give it to you." She cups my ear and whispers, "I'll give you all of me…I promise. But for now I want you to follow the Teacher. I'll meet you at the end of the month in the Holy City for the Great Festival. Will you do this for me?"

Imagining Maria and me together is sublime; I'd do anything to make it happen.

"Yes," I say, guilt descending into my soul. "But you must swear you'll come. Promise in the name of the one true God you'll be there."

"You have my word," she says. "Good things will happen in the Holy City, and then we'll be free. We'll start our life together. The Teacher is making all things new."

The guilt consumes me much faster than I expected. I thought I could explain our plan to Maria, make her understand why we must do what we will to the Teacher. But I see now she'd never understand. She's too enthralled by him to grasp the complexity of what it takes to liberate our people from oppression.

I take one more dig into Legion's hand then lie to her. "I'll follow faithfully and learn all I can from the Teacher. But then you and I will escape the South as soon as the Great Festival is over! Not a second later."

Maria kisses me, and I pray to God it won't be the last time I taste her lips. But I know it is.

Later that morning, I don't go to the Office of Record. Instead I continue to follow the Teacher and his twelve students; they've begun to emulate him in important ways since we left Geth Park. After the Teacher gave them authority, they've been able to teach with power and occasionally heal the sick. And they do it like the Teacher—instantly, miraculously.

Petra, in particular, has proven himself a fine leader. He's as Jude described him, fearless. I've been looking for a chance to speak with him in private, to inquire about his allegiances, but so far the opportunity hasn't presented itself.

The Teacher's plan, as far as I can tell, is to travel and teach for a few weeks before setting out for the Holy City and the Great Festival. The Great Festival is the holiest of all our holidays. All the faithful attend with their families. As the Teacher is a holy man, it's especially critical that he attend the Great Festival. Should he choose not to, Jude and I have been charged with the task of getting him there.

We're more than capable.

But storm clouds are gathering. Miles and a few others believe that once the Teacher reaches the Holy City, he'll finally unveil his plan to overthrow the Kingdom. Miles thinks that even though the Teacher has advocated a peaceful resistance, his position will change during the Great Festival, when more Americans will be gathered than any other time of the year. There he will capitalize upon his growing fame to strike hard and fast against the Kingdom.

While this idea intrigues me, I doubt it will happen. During my short time with the Teacher, I've seen nothing that leads me to believe he'll gather an army. Besides, he doesn't need to, because Jude and I already have taken care of it. We'll do what needs to be done to win freedom while the rest of these men sit around and talk philosophy.

But the real reason I don't pay much attention to the Teacher's plans is because I know something he doesn't.

He'll be locked in prison before the festival's end.

# CHAPTER 17

L ife on the road isn't half bad. The days are interesting, and the nights are quite fun. For a holy man, the Teacher is a surprisingly freewheeling fellow. He and his students rarely fast from food or drink, as the other religious authorities often do. Plus you never know what he'll say or do next. And I like that. If I'm honest, I've found myself enjoying the Teacher more with each passing day.

Jude says it's only natural to find him an attractive figure. After all, he gives so much to so many without asking for anything in return. But Jude also reminds me that I must keep in mind the ultimate goal and understand that his demise is necessary if we're to rise in rebellion.

I try to convince myself of this, but it's difficult to believe this about a man who's beloved by thousands. He literally breathes life into the lifeless and offers hope to the downtrodden. He's a hard man to hate.

But our plan is set. The men have abandoned their hiding place in the leper colony and are making their secret journey to the Holy City. So now there's nothing for Jude and me to do but make sure the Teacher arrives on time.

Frankly I could think of worse ways to wait out the revolution. Watching the Teacher stir up trouble is fun. Today has been no different—a full day of teaching and healing. The day has been so hectic that the Teacher, who's typically cheerful, looks exhausted. This morning I had a moment alone with him, and I nearly asked if I could do anything for him but then thought better of it. I can be close to him…but not that close.

The sun has set, and we've already prepared camp for the evening when the religious authorities from the Holy City arrive. One of them, a man with a fat belly hidden beneath a red robe, says, "Teacher, we've come from the Holy City, having heard of your wise counsel."

The Teacher greets them warmly.

Fat Belly says, "We know you've done great works today, many of which we saw with our own eyes, but we have a few questions for you, if it's not too much trouble."

The Teacher smiles, but I can see how weary he is. He looks as though he might topple over at any moment. "As you wish," he says.

This "questioning" from the authorities has come to be somewhat of a routine. These men are often angry with the Teacher because he teaches without having been properly ordained by our religious authorities. Like me, they're suspicious of his motives and often come to challenge his understanding of the Scripture. The other students get nervous about these encounters, but I love them because the Teacher has proven himself a great debater. More often than not, he confounds even the most learned of these men with his unorthodox responses. It's a fantastic show.

Fat Belly says, "Why do the students of the Baptist fast, but your students do not fast?"

Petra snickers loudly at the irony of the question. "When's the last time you missed a meal, old man?"

The Teacher shoots an annoyed glance at Petra. "The wedding guests can't fast while the bridegroom is with them, can they? As long as they have the bridegroom with them, they can't fast. The day will come when the bridegroom is taken away from them, and then they will fast on that day."

The religious authorities argue among themselves over what the Teacher means by this, then ask, "Why do your students not live according to the tradition of the elders but eat with defiled hands?" The man asking this question gestures toward Miles and me; we're drinking wine and grilling chickens over a small fire.

The man is right. It's true that we don't follow the age-old customs of our religion out here on the road. It's simply not practical to wash our dishes and our hands according to the tradition we were taught in our youth. We Southerners are a people deeply entrenched in our ways, but here—with the Teacher—we've lived with a bohemian sort of freedom that I find exhilarating. But the authorities have a valid point. What we're doing flies in the face of our religion, of our rich heritage.

The Teacher says, "The prophets were right about you hypocrites. You abandon the commandment of God and hold on to human traditions."

The authorities holler in protest, arguing that the Teacher is the hypocrite, for he violates the law. The Teacher says, "Listen to me, all of you, and understand—there's nothing outside a person that can defile him by going inside him. The things that come out are what defile. Do you not see that whatever goes into a person from outside cannot defile, since it enters not the heart but the stomach? What comes out of a person is what defiles, for it is from within, from the human heart, that evil comes: fornication, murder, theft, adultery, avarice, wickedness, deceit, licentiousness, envy, slander, pride, and folly. All these evils come from within, and they defile a person."

The authorities gasp in horror. It's unthinkable to them that the Teacher can dismiss tradition so easily. They turn away to argue among themselves, trying to decipher the Teacher's words. The Teacher joins us at the fire, as he often does before departing for prayer.

We drink wine and eat, and do our best to ignore the religious authorities who return to declare they'll follow and watch the Teacher closely in the coming days. They make a separate camp for themselves nearby. Thank God.

We quietly discuss the events of the day for another hour, and then, when we're full with meat and wine, the Teacher departs for the evening. He ventures deep into the wilderness, where he will pray until the sunrise.

Two things happen the following week. First, I miss Maria so badly that I can hardly stand it. Second, I see the Teacher do things no man can do. And yet...he does them anyway.

A deaf man hears his own voice for the first time.

A twelve-year-old girl dies. And then she wakes up.

A bleeding woman is healed by reaching out and taking hold of the Teacher's clothes. The Teacher tells us later her faith made her well. *Her faith.*

Crowds of four thousand people endure the grueling heat to listen to the Teacher all day long. In the evening, when there's nothing to eat but seven loaves of bread, every mouth is fed.

A blind man sees.

A paralyzed man receives the freedom of movement. But perhaps even more astonishing, the Teacher forgives his sins, which settles the matter for the religious authorities; the Teacher is a blasphemer, they believe, for only God can forgive sins. They declare only one suitable penalty for a blasphemer: death.

Then the Teacher asks us a question that changes everything. "Who do people say I am?" The fourteen of us are walking alone when the question comes. There are no masses of people, only us, his students.

For a time no one says anything. Then I speak up. "They say you're a prophet. Perhaps one of the great ones returned from the grave?"

The other students echo my thoughts. They all agree the people see him as the Son of Man, sent from heaven to save the people from the tyranny of King Charles's kingdom.

The Teacher stops walking and listens to our replies. He presses us further. "But who do you say I am?"

Petra answers first, with fire in his voice. "You...are...the...messiah."

The Teacher's eyes give him away. I turn sharply to Jude, who keeps his focus trained squarely on the Teacher, clearly anxious to hear his reply.

But the Teacher says nothing to indicate whether Petra is correct. Instead he says, "Say nothing more of this."

"But," Petra begins, "we must—"

"What you must understand is that the Son of Man will undergo great suffering and be rejected by the elders, the chief priests, and the scribes, and be killed and after three days rise again."

Petra takes the Teacher by his shoulders and forcefully leads him away from the group. It's the first time I've seen anyone handle him this way. In private Petra speaks harsh words to the Teacher. They argue madly over what the Teacher has just said.

"Get behind me, Evil One!" the Teacher yells. "For you are setting your mind not on divine things but on human things." Then he calls to all of us, "If any want to become my followers, let them deny themselves and take up their cross and follow me, for those who want to save their life will lose it, and those who lose their life for my sake, and for the sake of the gospel, will save it. For what will it profit them to gain the whole world and forfeit their life?"

No one dares offer a reply. His words stun us into silence.

The Teacher spends the night alone in prayer while the rest of us debate the meaning of what he has said. I say, "Must you die to be the Teacher's follower? Is this what he has in mind for all of you…death on a Kingdom cross? Is that where his "way" leads?"

Petra shakes his head violently. "It can't be! No! That's why I got so upset with him. I don't want the Teacher talking that way. It's absurd! No one here will die when we reach the Holy City. We've worked and struggled for too long. This will be a time of victory, not defeat. The only people who will die will be those who side with the Kingdom. End of story."

"Yes," Miles says, "but I'm beginning to wonder if the Teacher's notion of victory is different than ours. I'd thought he'd change his tactics by now. We're only days away from the festival, and still he makes no preparation for battle. We spend every waking moment with the poor, feeding widows, healing the lame. I don't protest these righteous actions, but at some point we must set our sights on higher things."

"Yes," I say. "This may sound crude, but freedom can't be won out here with the weak. It'll only be won in the city, where power resides. The message must be brought to the Holy City and the seat of power. The people may love the Teacher, but these aren't the crowds the Kingdom is afraid of. The Teacher spends his time and energy focusing on the wrong kinds of people."

Miles sighs. "I wish Maria were with us. She would understand the Teacher; she can always interpret his intentions."

The men raise their glasses in a toast to Maria. Everyone drinks, but no one is happy.

"The religious authorities shouldn't be dismissed so easily," I say. "It's a mistake. He's already broken the law in their eyes. I've heard whispers."

"Of what?" Petra asks.

"Of death. They say he heals by the power of Satan and commits blasphemy when he forgives the sins of prostitutes and tax collectors. Not even our most esteemed prophets have claimed this authority. Only God can forgive sin."

The mood of the evening sours to an irrevocable point, causing the students to disband. Each man wanders away from the fire to sleep alone in the darkness. Eventually only Petra and I are left sitting by the flames. I seize the opportunity, saying, "You've begun to doubt his methods, haven't you?"

Petra sighs deeply. "I have...or at least I did. I'm not ashamed to admit it. I'm just a man, not a prophet like the Baptist. But something happened that convinced me otherwise," Petra says.

I flinch. "What? What happened?"

"It was late. All of you were sleeping. The Teacher woke me up. He took Miles, John, and me up onto the mountain. We followed for an hour in silence, with no idea where we were going. When we reached the top of our climb, he was transfigured before us."

"Transfigured?"

"His clothes became a dazzling white, such as no one on earth could bleach them."

"How could that be?"

"And then, standing before us, were the two great prophets of our religion, talking with the Teacher."

"The great prophets have been dead for ages! How could you have seen them?"

Petra gazes into the fire, transfixed by the whipping flames and crackling wood. "I have no idea. The three of us were terrified. We didn't know what to say or do. But it was marvelous because the Teacher finally looked like the king we knew he is. He was radiant, emitting such power that King Charles himself would bow had he seen him." Petra looks directly at me and says, "That's when I was convinced—convinced to follow the Teacher wherever and however he leads. He's truly the Christ, our anointed one."

I say nothing. After a long beat of silence, I stand up and throw a bucket of water on Petra's fire. Then I stalk away into the night.

# CHAPTER 18

I find the Teacher on his knees. He's deep in prayer on the bank of a nearby river. I turn sharply in another direction, but he calls out to me before I escape. "Can't sleep?" he says.

"No. Not tonight."

"Join me in me prayer, won't you?" I walk to where he's praying and kneel on the ground. The river flows calmly before us, and I try to let its beauty ease my anxiety. It doesn't work. The Teacher says, "At a river like this, the Baptist anointed me."

"Were you his student?"

"I went to him and was baptized for the forgiveness of sin, as our religion requires."

"What sin did you have, Teacher? If there were ever a righteous man, it is you. You condemn no one, not even the greatest of sinners."

"The Son of Man came to offer himself for the sins of many," he says. "We're all brothers and sisters, Deacon. It was good for the Baptist to cleanse me in the water, for I've come to be the firstborn of a new creation. I've come to lead us back to God."

I nod and pretend I understand him then change the subject. "You looked troubled today. Are you tired from the travel? I know the crowds have made it difficult for you to rest."

The Teacher grins. "You can see I'm troubled?"

"Only Miles smiles more than you. But today…you didn't look right."

"Miles." The Teacher grins again. "He's a happy man, isn't he?"

"He's a good man."

The Teacher nods, looks at the river, and allows his grin to disappear into its waters. "My friend is dead," he says.

"Who?"

"The Baptist, my cousin and mentor; the governor had him executed. My father died when I was young. The Baptist took it upon himself to make a man of me. He prepared the way for my ministry and for me. I owed him everything."

"I'm...sorry for your loss." We sit in silence and listen to the flowing river, the trickle of water running across the rocks in the shallows. An owl, high in the trees above, hoots softly. "My parents recently passed," I tell him. "I share in your grief."

The Teacher reaches out and squeezes my shoulder. "Thank you."

"What happened to the Baptist?" I ask. "Why was he in prison?"

"The American governor of the South, who's in cahoots with the Kingdom, had him arrested."

"His crime?"

"Telling the truth. The Baptist was put in chains for nothing more than acting as a genuine prophet of the one true God. There was no crime. The governor is supposed to be a man who follows the one true God, but he stole his brother's wife and took her in marriage. The Baptist informed him this was unlawful and spoke publicly about the sin of this action. But the governor is a prideful man and didn't want to hear it. So he arrested the Baptist. His new wife was looking for an excuse to do away with him ever since."

"I'm surprised the governor waited so long. There was no law stopping his execution. The Kingdom wouldn't have interfered. They despise any Southerner who gains a following that might challenge their authority."

"Very true, but the governor feared the Baptist. He knew he was a righteous and holy man, so he protected him. The governor is an intellectual, and he loved to listen to the Baptist preach. He reveled in the challenge of trying to discern his perplexing sermons."

"Then why have him killed?"

"Because even smart men don't always think with their brains." He winks at me. "I believe you know what I'm talking about."

"I do," I say, nervous.

"Maria is unlike any woman I've known," the Teacher says. "A rare bird."

"Do you love her?" I say. "Sometimes I think every man here does."

The Teacher laughs. "You may be right about that. Look, Deacon, you need to make up your mind about your intentions."

"With what?"

"Maria."

I try hard not to show it, but my heart is lodged in my throat. I'm terrified that I may have to restrain the Teacher right here and now. Finally I say, "I don't understand."

"You have to make a decision. You must choose."

"Between…what?" I say, readying myself to jump him.

"Love and war."

"You're not making sense to me."

The Teacher's voice turns hard. "Either take Maria away from here or do what you came to do. You can't have both."

I don't know understand how the Teacher can know this. It's as if he knows my soul better than I do. Sometimes I catch him looking at me, and I'm certain he's discovered our plan. But if he did—if he truly understood our betrayal— he would do something about it. Why would he allow Jude and me to be here? This thought soothes me.

"Tell me what happened to the Baptist," I say, once again trying to change the subject. "I want to know how they killed him."

The Teacher looks out at the river as he speaks. "There was a party for the governor's birthday. All the Southern officers and officials gathered for the celebration. The daughter of the governor's new wife danced before the entire banquet. She was beautiful, and the governor was enchanted. Like I said, men don't always think with their brains. When she finished dancing, the governor said she could have anything she wanted, up to half his kingdom. So the girl rushed out of the party and asked her mother what she ought to request. And her mother said, 'The head of the Baptist.'"

"But the governor feared him?"

The Teacher laughs grimly. "You've been out West too long. The rulers in the South are nothing if not barbaric, Deacon. This is a government of domi- nation. I'm told the governor was grieved, but he had no choice but to keep his oath. There were too many witnesses; he couldn't afford to lose face."

"So he sent in the order?"

"Within the hour the Baptist's head was brought on a platter into the banquet hall and presented to the young dancer, who then took it to her mother."

"Unbelievable."

"Like I said, you need to choose between love or war. Don't drag Maria into anything you'll regret. The Baptist's death is a sign of what's coming... perhaps for us all."

"Was he given a proper burial?"

"Yes. His students retrieved the body from prison and placed it in a tomb. Then came to give me the news."

"So his soul traveled peacefully to the afterlife?"

The Teacher nods.

"Good," I say.

"No," he says bitterly. "It's not good." His face is stressed in a way I haven't seen it before. Dark lines run across his forehead, and vertical grooves cut down the sides of his cheeks. Suddenly the Teacher looks much older than before, as if this outburst of fame has aged him in unnatural and hurried ways. He draws a heavy breath then stares up to the heavens.

And then he's crying, hard and deep sobs of despair, the sort of tears I shed for my parents. Before I can help it, I'm crying too; both of us are crumbling like distraught children.

That's all that's said this night. There's nothing else but the sound of two men weeping over the intolerable cruelty of the grave.

# CHAPTER 19

I weep hard for my parents until I fall asleep on the bank of the river. Then I dream of Maria.

Even though I haven't physically laid eyes on her since she left with Legion, she's come to me every night in my dreams. She laughs, her black eyes sparkling like onyx. She throws back her long hair and sings to me. I chase her through a field of wildflowers, and we fall softly to the earth, our arms and legs tangling around each other's bodies.

We kiss. We kiss some more. Then we get older. I see a baby at her breast, then another. Both children have my blue eyes—the eyes of my mother. I finish school in Mexico and become a doctor for our small community. It's a good life, a peaceful life. I tend to the aches of the body; I meet the needs of the people. Our children grow up bright and lovely under a forever golden sky. They adore their mother and think I'm the strongest man in the world—which, had I not abandoned my people, I might have been.

But then the beast comes. Like a dragon with iron teeth, it rips our family apart, forcing me away to fight a war I care nothing about. My children wail, falling to the ground in tears. Maria screams and beats on the chests of the centurions who've come to take me away.

I'm thrown on a train and taken north.

And then I wake up.

Jude stands where the Teacher was sleeping. "You must go to the Office of Record today," he says. "It can't be put off any longer. You've already missed one Monday meeting. Miss another and a warrant will be issued for your arrest."

I rub my eyes and sit up awkwardly, my joints stiff from another night on the hard earth. The sun is just beginning its climb into the sky, but the air is already heavy with heat. "We need my money before going to the Holy City?"

"It's the price demanded by Henrik. The Nordic wants to be paid first."

"I should have killed him when I had the chance."

"You did enough damage. The men sent word that he still can't chew solid food. We're lucky he hasn't changed his mind. You should thank the gods he's still willing to help our cause."

"I have difficulty trusting a man I have to bribe." I stand up and stretch my arms and legs. "And you mean, 'thank the one true God,' don't you?"

Jude rolls his eyes. "Whatever. Take the Ducati and go. You can make it to Oxford and return here by nightfall. The Teacher already has said we won't move from this place today. The crowds gathering are already massive. He'll teach, and then we'll rest one more night before we begin our journey. This is it, Deacon. It's happening. Everything we hoped for is about to take place. The revolution has begun."

I don't like Jude. I know my father did, but I don't. Something about him bothers me. I've tried to shake the feeling, telling myself it's paranoia, but it won't go away. I'm grateful for him, for his planning and his organization, but I don't like him. Even so, I need him. And necessity, like friendship, can be that simple.

"I'll go," I say, "but I've been thinking about the Teacher."

Jude laughs. "You and the rest of the South. What can I say? He's the most famous man in a generation. The religious authorities are right to want him silenced. Who knows what he'll say next?"

"I...think...I don't know. Maybe he can be useful to our movement."

"Give me a break." Jude spits and rolls his eyes again. "Am I going to have to listen to you sing his praises too?"

"It's just that he helps so many. And he does have power. You can't deny it. Your eyes have seen the same things I've seen. He's a doer of mighty deeds, Jude."

Jude wants to dismiss with me. He wants nothing more than to tell me to shut up and forget about this nonsense. But something in my voice tells him that would be a mistake.

He exhales then says, "Listen, Deacon. The Teacher is special. Only an idiot would deny it. But that doesn't mean he's who the people say he is." He takes a furtive look around and lowers his voice. "He's *not* the messiah. *You are*. The messiah must lead an army. You have an army. The messiah must shed the blood of his enemies. You've already proven yourself capable of that. The messiah must have resources—you *do*!" Jude takes a shallow breath. "The Teacher is a good, good man. No one doubts that. He cares for every soul he meets. And yes, he works miracles, but he's only a *teacher*. For the sake of all the gods! He's a spirit person; his place is out here teaching people to love God. But our place—the men who'll restore our nation—is in the Holy City, with blood on our hands. It takes a special kind of man to do such a thing, and that isn't the Teacher. It's you."

"But he speaks of ushering in the kingdom of God, Jude. He says that the time is fulfilled, that the time has finally come. He proclaims the ages ending! Don't you see? There's so much about him that fits the prophecies of our ancestors."

Jude picks up a smooth stone from the ground and rolls it around in his hands. "Five thousand men depend on you. Five thousand men are marching toward the Holy City, prepared to fight and die in your name. This is the first chance our people have had at freedom in years. Abandon them now, and that chance surely will be lost—this time for who knows how long. Are you prepared to risk that? I mean, for what—a few miracles in the wilderness? Come on!"

"Miles told me about the Teacher's birth. Have you heard?"

Jude throws the stone across the water. It skips three times before disappearing beneath the surface, sinking to the muddy bottom where it'll stay for a hundred years. "I've heard the rumors about the virgin, if that's what you mean. I doubt it's true."

"That's not what I'm talking about."

"Enlighten me then." Jude looks up to the sun. "But we don't have all morning. You need to get moving."

"Wise men from the Far East came to witness his birth because they'd read about the promise of a messiah in the Scripture. The Southern governor heard about their journey and tried to find out where the Teacher was born. But the wise men wouldn't tell him where the exact birthplace was—only the town. They had to give him something to avoid being killed. Infuriated, the governor sent orders for all the children under the age of two in that town to be killed. *Children*, Jude. Babies were massacred that night. Hundreds of them."

"Have you lost your mind? All Southern children are told that story. There was an outbreak in the town, a terrible infection that had to be eradicated. There was no other choice."

"I knew that story was a lie, knew it the first time my mother told it to me."

"It's not a lie!"

"It is. That governor knew then what the people know now!"

"Which is?"

"The messiah has come."

"Now that, Deacon, is true!" Jude takes my face in his hands, and I'm too overcome with emotion to shake him off. "The messiah has come. I'm looking right at him."

I take the deepest breath of my life and say, "I pray to God you're right."

I reach the Office of Record by noon. I park the Ducati and march into the lobby, where I demand to see Dr. Stone. During my journey here, I've replayed Jude's words a thousand times in my head. If it is true that I'm the one who will free the people, it's time I started acting like it. And if I'm God's anointed one, I have nothing to fear—especially not from some crazy psychologist.

Upon my arrival, I'm escorted immediately to Dr. Stone's office. She's writing in cursive at her desk when I enter. I sit in the same chair as before, this time without being invited. The good doctor doesn't look up until I prop my boots on her desk and kick a few heavy books to the floor.

"Oops," I say.

"Well," she says coolly, "look what we have here."

"I need to authorize a man named Jude Iscariot to withdraw funds from my account at the Oxford Trust. Will that be a problem?"

Dr. Stone slides her glasses off her nose, folds them in her hands, and says, "Not at all." She smiles. "I can have it done before the day's end. Anything else I can do for you, Your Highness?"

I pull my feet from her desk and sit up straight in the chair, trying not to look absolutely shocked by her answer. "That...should do it, thanks."

Dr. Stone swings her chair around to a filing cabinet and withdraws an official-looking form. "I'll need your signature, of course." She places the paper on her desk and points to the bottom line. She offers me her pen.

I stand and take the pen in my hand. She watches carefully as I sign my name. "Is that it?"

"Not quite," she says slowly. "There's another matter we ought to discuss."

I swallow hard, my mind flashing back to Dr. Stone's hands wrapped tightly around my neck. "What?"

Her mouth twitches before she says, "I gave you explicit instructions."

"And here I am, reporting for duty, ma'am." I give her a two-fingered salute.

"One." She points her index finger at me. "You attacked two Kingdom guardsmen, giving one of the men a concussion that landed him in hospital. Two." Another finger jumps out at me. "You resisted arrest and took leave underground with a woman known for associating with demoniacs and other bandits. Three..." The ring finger comes out. "You missed your required meeting last Monday. Four..." The pinkie. "You've been seen cavorting with this Southern teacher who openly speaks of a coming kingdom, committing treason everywhere he goes. And five..." Her thumb rounds out my offenses. "You sit here in *my* office and treat me like some kind of hired servant who does your bidding. Did I miss anything?"

My throat clenches. I knew Dr. Stone would know about the incident at the bank. And it's conceivable the guards could have described Maria with some accuracy. But how she knows everything else is beyond me.

Then it hits me.

If she knows about Maria, then she's been in danger ever since I left her here in Oxford. That's when the roof comes down. *They already have her.* A cold sweat breaks across my body.

"What's wrong, Deacon? Lost for words?"

My body trembles. "Have you hurt her?"

"Why don't you have a seat so we can get a few things straight?" Her mouth twitches again. "I've missed you, Deacon Larsen."

I fall into the chair with a thud, my mind and body numbed by the thought that the Kingdom has taken Maria prisoner. Surely Legion would have put up a fight. He may hate me, but he'd die for Maria. He wouldn't go down easily.

Dr. Stone says, "You won't see me after today."

"Why not?" I ask slowly.

"Aren't you planning to travel to the Holy City for the Great Festival, as your people call it?"

"I'm sorry," I say, rubbing my eyes with the heels of my hands. "How do you know all this? And please tell me what you've done to Maria. You don't understand—I love her."

Dr. Stone issues a hallow laugh that drips in cruelty. "*You love her?*" she says spitefully.

"With all my heart."

"Maria Magdalena isn't the kind of woman a man loves, Deacon. Well, not for longer than a night." She laughs at her joke and adds, "But I'm sure you know all about that. At least I pray someone's told you about her sullied reputation."

"You wouldn't talk like that if you knew what was good for you."

Dr. Stone rises from her desk like a geyser bursting. "And you wouldn't treat me like a dog if you knew what was good for you!"

I jump out of my seat. "You're not the only one in this office with power, lady. And you're testing my patience. Now tell me what you've done with Maria—I won't ask again."

"Why do you think you're not already in chains on a northbound train? Have you thought for a good moment about that? How on King Charles's holy earth have you not been arrested for your crimes, you slobbering little brat?"

"I'm warning you, woman—"

"Warning me?" she cackles. "Poor me!" She puts a hand over her mouth in exaggerated horror. "The baby is warning me! What am I to do?" She drops her voice an octave. "I'm the only reason you're not dead—the *only* reason."

"That's not true. Maria saved my life. And Jude is the one who—"

"Jude lives because I say he lives. He breathes by the mercy of my good graces and nothing more!"

117

"What are you talking about?"

"You get so far ahead of yourself for someone so young, Deacon. I fear you won't last long in this war. But that's not really my concern, is it?"

"What are you talking about?"

"I know everything, son—*everything*. And I hear you're getting cold feet. What's wrong, Deacon? Can't handle the heat now that the fight draws near?"

My head feels light as a balloon. I fall back into the chair to avoid passing out. Then I slowly say, "You're a part of the resistance?"

That horrible cackle again. "God, no!" she screams. "Of course not. What do you take me for…a complete idiot? Do you think I have a death wish?"

"But—"

"But we all do what we have to do. What? You think Henrik is the only Kingdom loyalist who brokers deals with you Americans? Your delivery of the Teacher into our hands will prove very profitable for me." She smiles that wicked smile again. "I plan to retire soon. This deal will allow me to leave this wretched country and go home and live the sort of life I richly deserve."

"And you're OK with what we plan to do—"

"Stop talking!" She covers her ears. "I don't want to hear another word about it. I have no clue what else you lunatics have planned, and I don't care. All that matters to me is that Jude can withdraw the funds in your account and that you get the Teacher to the Holy City on time. That's it."

"What if I don't?"

Dr. Stone smirks. She retrieves another file and flops it open on her desk. Inside is a black-and-white photo of Maria and Alejandro. They're lying on a blanket in the middle of a park. The park looks dangerously familiar. A flash of memory from our one magical night goes off in my head. "This photo was taken yesterday," Dr. Stone says. "If you go anywhere but directly back to the Teacher, Maria will be arrested and executed on the spot. I'll see to it myself. I'll be sure to take a picture of that for you as well. Think it's hard seeing her with another man? Trying erasing the image of her bloody corpse from your brain."

"No," I say. "*Please* don't do that."

"It's not up to me. You hold the power."

"Fine. You can trust me. You have my signature. Jude will pay you in full. I swear the Teacher will be in the Holy City for the Great Festival. You can count on me."

"Once you're there, we'll need to know his exact whereabouts. Jude knows the details."

"Whatever you want," I say, glaring hard at the photo of Maria.

Dr. Stone looks at the picture. "She's a beautiful woman. I see why you've fallen so hard, even if she's been had by many, many men. I've known her for years. It was me who denied her visa." I don't look up from the photo or respond to Dr. Stone, but I know she's smiling. "But do you know what's really interesting, Deacon? In all the time I've known her, I don't believe I've ever seen her happier than she is in that photo."

Dr. Stone taps her long fingernails on the glossy photo and laughs again.

# CHAPTER 20

I'm back in the countryside before sunset.

In the twilight I discover the largest group yet. Thousands have come to hear the Teacher. As I wade through the crowds, I hear people gossiping about him. Many praise the Teacher, calling him the true messiah, come at long last. Others debate whether his power comes from the one true God or the Evil One. Still others are confused, or curious to catch a glimpse of the man who performs many inexplicable deeds.

It takes another hour before I reach the twelve students and the Teacher. That's how large the crowd has become.

When I finally arrive, people are bringing small children to the Teacher so he might touch them with a blessing. But Petra and Jude push the parents away, trying to protect the Teacher from this crowd that could easily morph into a dangerous mob. It's an unsafe scene. The Teacher has many enemies, and more religious authorities are gathered here than ever before. Their hatred for the Teacher is written across their faces; it's no longer enough that he be silenced. They seem to wish something far more sinister to befall him.

When the Teacher realizes what Petra and Miles are doing, he becomes indignant. "Let the little children come to me!" he cries out. "Do not stop them, for it is such as these that the kingdom of God belongs. Truly I tell you, whoever doesn't receive the kingdom of God as a little child will never enter it."

Petra and Miles obediently stand down, which allows the children to break free and run recklessly toward the Teacher, tiny arms flailing, laughter rising high in the air. The Teacher swoops them in his arms and lifts them up for all to see. "Whoever wants to be first must be last of all and servant of all. Whoever welcomes one such child in my name welcomes me, and whoever welcomes me welcomes not me but the one who sent me." Even as the crowd balloons to an uncontrollable size, the Teacher takes another hour to bless each and every little one who comes to him. There's a happy glow to the children's faces when they skip back to their parents.

After the last child scurries away, a man breaks free from the crowd and rushes at the Teacher. He is dressed in a fine linen suit and has an entourage of men who follow closely after him. Miles and Petra lurch forward to stop him, but it's too late; the entourage blocks them.

When he reaches the Teacher, he stops abruptly and falls to his knees, his face to the ground. I've seen many poor people out here following the Teacher, but this is the first time an apparently wealthy man has humbled himself in such dramatic fashion. "Good Teacher," the rich man says, "what must I do to inherit eternal life?"

No one ever asked this question before. A blanket of silence falls over the crowd of thousands. The only audible noise is the chirping of the crickets and the excited breathing of so many humans gathered in one place.

"Why do you call me 'good'?" the Teacher replies. "No one is good but God alone. You know the commandments: 'You shall not murder; you shall not commit adultery; you shall not steal; you shall not bear false witness; you shall not defraud; honor your father and mother…'"

The man lifts his head and declares proudly, "Teacher, I've kept all these since my youth."

"You lack one thing; go, sell what you own, and give the money to the poor, and you will have treasure in heaven. Then come. Follow me."

At this the crickets seem to stop chirping, as does our collective breathing. I've never heard such a deafening silence in all my life. Everyone, including the Teacher, anxiously awaits the man's response.

Slowly the man rises from his knees and pats out the wrinkles and dust from his expensive suit. Then, painfully, he turns back to his entourage and motions for them to leave. A smile spreads across the Teacher's face. But then the man turns and follows his entourage. He keeps his eyes low as he walks. The crowd erupts in a horrified gasp.

The man, like the Teacher's smile, is gone as quickly as he came.

The Teacher addresses the crowd. His eyes are watery. "How hard will it be for those who have wealth to enter the kingdom of God?" Another gasp arises from the crowd. "Children, how hard it is to enter the kingdom of God! It is easier for a camel to go through the eye of a needle than for someone who is rich to enter the kingdom of God."

A random voice from the crowd shouts out, "Then who can be saved? Tell us, Teacher! Please tell us! Show us how! Light the way!"

The Teacher spins around, addressing the crowd encircling him. He cries in a loud voice, "For mortals it is impossible, but not for God. For God all things are possible!"

"But Teacher!" Petra cries back. "We've left everything and followed you!"

"Truly I tell you, there's no one who has left his house or brothers or sisters or mother or father or children or fields, for my sake and for the sake of the good news, who will not receive a hundredfold now in this age: houses, brothers, and sisters, mothers and children, and fields, with persecutions—and in the age to come...*eternal life.* But many who are first will be last, and the last will be first."

At these words the crowd ignites into a full-fledged frenzy. Some shout with joy. Others call out to the Teacher, begging for clarification. "We don't understand!" they scream. "What does this mean?" Others lash out in anger, howling, "Only God can grant eternal life! How can you claim such a thing! It's a blasphemy! This is blasphemy!"

In the end all the angry and confused voices are drowned out by a unified and earth-shattering chant. It brings me to my knees in fear. With a passion worthy of the angels attending the one true God in heaven, the people roar, "Messiah! Messiah! Messiah!"

Sleep doesn't come easy to me tonight. I toss and turn for hours, awakening from countless nightmares. I'm tempted to get up, awake the Teacher, and demand an answer from him. I want to know what he has planned, and I want to hear it in plain language.

*Are you or are you not going to fight the Kingdom?*

How complicated can it be? I need an answer; I have to know exactly what he wants to do. Enough with all this talk—it's time for action.

These people in the countryside believe the Teacher is the anointed one of God. Thousands of them plan to follow us into the Holy City for the Great Festival. It will be a sight to see. Thousands of Americans will come to the

Holy City to worship the one true God, with two men being called the messiah. There's a buzz in the air, with people saying the time finally has come, that this is it—the ages are finally ending.

There have been whispers, even here, that a Southerner has returned home and is marching an army toward the Holy City. But no one knows his name. There are many rumors. He is the Son of Man coming with the clouds of heaven, riding a white horse, and carrying a bloodied sword. He's a dragon with ten heads who spits fire from his mouth, able to scorch King Charles's army in a single hour. He's very young, they say—just a student returned home to save his people. He is neither an angel nor a dragon but simply a man touched by God.

I say nothing to anyone but Jude, who tells me to listen to the people and believe their words. "They know the truth about you, Deacon, and soon the whole world will also. When the army reaches the Holy City and you assume command, they all will know the truth—the messiah has come and is everything they've heard. You're the Son of Man, a dragon from hell, and a warrior. The man who carries the gun of his rebel father. The man who'll cut off the head of our dreaded enemy."

But still I doubt. It's been a long while since I heard the men chant "Messiah" for me. Even then, it was only one night—so very fast, like a dream. I went to them. I battled the Nordic, beating him senseless, and they hoisted me like a king and revealed to me their plan.

King Charles will make an unannounced visit to the Holy City for the Great Festival. No one knows he's coming. Henrik, our Centurion Guard traitor, is apparently a high-ranking soldier with access to top-secret information and to the king himself. King Charles is smart enough to realize the calls for rebellion have grown too loud in the South. His presence at the Great Festival will send a strong message to those calling for war. Henrik says the king plans on executing a record number of criminals on Kingdom crosses, just to make sure he gets his point across.

My army will wait outside the city wall until they receive my signal.

When the king visits a royal territory, it's his custom to meet the families of those "selected" for work in the camps. It's a public display of honor, a chance for the king to praise loyal service and courage. When a family member has perished in the camps, as both my mine have, the king humbles himself by kissing the hand of a surviving relative.

Here's the important part. Because weapons have been banned for so many years in the South, there's no serious need to check Kingdom subjects for guns, unless there's good suspicion to do so. According to Henrik, if I keep close to him, I'm all but assured to go unchecked. Which means no one will know that when the king bends down to kiss my hand, I'm going to blow off his head.

# CHAPTER 21

We rise early the next morning and begin our journey to the Holy City. It is a full day's walk if you move fast and don't stop for food. But given the enormous size of our group, the trip will take two days. The Teacher believes it's important that we move as one cohesive unit, not leaving anyone behind—a difficult task when thousands are in tow.

The debates from the night before have continued in the daylight. Some follow because they're in awe of the Teacher and expect great things to happen in the Holy City. Others are terrified of what could happen when thousands of Americans pour into the city hailing the Teacher as the messiah. The Kingdom won't take this lightly.

The Kingdom reserves its harshest brutality for men who believe they can challenge authority. There have been countless other would-be messiahs in the past, all of whom met violent deaths. It's telling that there are no old men in our midst who tell stories from days when they called themselves messiahs. A messiah either delivers his people or he's buried by his people. There's no other way.

Petra and Miles spend much of the morning in intense argument over what should be done in the Holy City. Both men show signs of cracking under the mounting stress. We're all too aware of what our journey to the Holy City represents. Out here in the countryside, we haven't yet reached the point of no return. Anyone of us could simply withdraw from the Teacher and be swallowed into the herd and be lost and gone forever. There's no one and nothing stopping us. The choice is still ours.

But should we enter the city limits with him and these people cheering for their new messiah, all bets are off. Even Petra, whom I believe doesn't experience fear as a normal man does, looks timid.

Around noon our fears are compounded. We've just climbed out of a deep valley when we come upon a mass execution. We see fifty Kingdom crosses perched atop a hill, with a dead man nailed to each one. It's an atrocious sight, and mothers work hard to cover the faces of their children, but it's impossible to shield them from the horror. The carnage is nauseating.

These poor souls have been dead for days. The scavengers of the sky already have done their work to the corpses and moved on to the next feeding ground. Eyeballs are missing from sockets. Limbs have been gnawed to the bone. One man's heart dangles from his open chest. There's so much dried blood on the men's bodies that they look like creatures from another world—a world inhabited by skinned humans.

The nails have been driven through both arms and the feet. Many of the legs are badly broken and disfigured. If a man survives long enough on the cross, the Kingdom eventually will grant him one small act of mercy by breaking his legs. That way he can no longer push himself up to take in deep breaths and will die much faster. It's the only act of generosity in what is otherwise the most torturous means of death devised by man.

Our people are tired, but we can't stop for rest in this place. We push onward and promise the younger ones food once we've moved beyond this unholy gravesite.

"It's a warning," Petra says to me, "a warning for anyone traveling into the Holy City."

Miles points to the crosses. "Challenge the Kingdom's authority, and this is what happens to you."

"Look upon your fate, boys," I say. "That's what they want for us."

Jude comes alongside us. "No man deserves to die like this. It's beyond evil."

"They're all Southerners," I say. "You men realize that, right? These are our people who died like dogs—our people who've been denied proper burials. *Our* brothers' souls that are denied a peaceful pilgrimage to the afterlife."

Petra spits on the ground. "They'll pay for this! Every last one of them will pay for their sins. I'd gladly give my own life for it."

I also spit. "As would I!"

Miles and Jude both spit too.

126

I take a hard look at the crosses and allow the image to singe my brain. I want it there forever. I never want to forget what the Kingdom has done to my people. "The people are right," I say. "Our ages are ending. Let's kill them all."

After our midday rest, the Teacher pulls the twelve aside, including me, and speaks some kind of gibberish. "We're going to the Holy City, and the Son of Man will be handed over to the religious authorities, and they'll condemn him to death. Then they'll hand him over to the Kingdom. They'll mock him and spit upon him and flog him and kill him. After three days he'll rise again."

The Teacher is sweating profusely and looks very tired as he speaks. He searches us with piercing eyes but we all avoid eye contact because no one has any idea what he's saying. The entire situation is awkward, uncomfortable, and frankly inappropriate. Jude was right; he's no messiah.

Finally Petra proves brave enough to break the silence. "Teacher, we want you to do something for us."

The Teacher wipes sweat from his brow. "What is it?"

"Promise us that we'll sit at your right and at your left in glory. Assure us of our seats in power, once we reach the Holy City. We need this—all of us." Petra hesitates. "We need some guarantee we'll be given authority."

The Teacher bows his head and shakes it slowly. "You don't know what you're asking. "Do you think you're able to drink from the cup from which I drink, or be baptized in the baptismal waters in which I was baptized?"

"We're able," Miles replies. "All of us. We're ready. You've prepared us for it."

"The cup from which I drink you will drink from, and in the baptismal waters in which I was baptized, you will be baptized. You can rest assured of this. But to sit at my right or at my left—that's not mine to grant, but it is for those for whom it has been prepared."

"He's losing it," I whisper in Jude's ear. "The strain of it all is breaking him. The man is falling apart."

Jude and I watch in silence as an argument breaks out among Petra and Miles and the nine others. Petra and Miles force the issue, wheedling the Teacher for clarification and confirmation about their coming power. Petra wants control of the army, while Miles asks to be the minister of finance. The others beg for them to stop and leave the Teacher alone.

127

*He's had enough,* I think. *Can't they see it?*

The ridiculousness goes on for another ten minutes before the Teacher exhales deeply and says, "Enough!" The men fall silent. "You know that among the Kingdom those whom they recognize as their rulers lord it over them, and their great ones are tyrants over them. But it isn't so among you. Whoever wishes to become great must be your servant, and whoever wishes to be first among you must be the slave of all. For the Son of Man came not to be served but to serve and to give his life as a ransom for many."

"There you have it," I say under my breath. "The final straw. He's lost and gone forever."

Jude nods. "It's rather sad to watch a good man lose his mind. I've followed the Teacher for years, hoping he had a decent plan hidden up his sleeve. But this—to become servants? That's how he believes we'll become greater than King Charles and his mighty Kingdom? He's insane."

It's true. Even I hoped the Teacher might come around at the last hour and prove himself more useful than this. Deep down I dreamt wildly and foolishly that he might use his powers to come to our defense in battle. The man, after all, commands the wind and the sea. Imagine what he might do to the enemy, should he choose to. But no—every man has his breaking point. And it's painfully obvious the Teacher has arrived at his.

I take a long hard look at the Teacher and the men who've given up their lives to follow him. Then I take in the thousands who surround us: women, children, fathers, brothers, wives, sisters. My stomach turns sour. I say, "This man needs to travel back to Oxford to take his rest. He has no business leading a mass of sheep to slaughter."

I walk away, eager to be alone, and think of nothing but Maria's dark eyes and cocoa skin.

# CHAPTER 22

We reach the outskirts of the Holy City by midafternoon the following day. We're near a small mountain when the Teacher orders our group to stop walking. He sends Petra and Miles into the small village outside the Holy City with explicit instructions. "Go into the village ahead of us, and immediately when you enter it, you'll find a colt that has never been ridden. Untie it and bring it back. If anyone says, 'Why are you doing this?' just say, 'The Lord needs it and will send it back here immediately.'"

Petra and Miles exchange confused looks before scurrying away to do the Teacher's bidding. The rest of us use the hour to get off our feet and find shade to hide from the blazing sun.

I've just nodded off when Petra and Miles return with the colt. It's a beautiful animal; its muscles are sinewy and its mane jet black, reminding me of Maria. It's a colt without blemish, also like Maria.

During my short time with the Teacher, I've never seen him ride a colt or any other animal. He has never once elevated himself above the rest of us but has instead walked humbly among his loyal followers. But now he climbs atop this colt, says nothing of this dramatic change, and motions for us to continue our journey.

I hurry over to Petra and Miles. "What's going on?"

Miles and Petra are too transfixed on the unfolding scene to answer me. As the colt marches slowly forward, the sea of people parts in front of the Teacher, allowing him to cut down the center. Then, one by one, they bow. Men pull the clothing off their backs and lay it on the ground for the colt to trample. Others break palm branches from surrounding trees and wave them before the parade, saying, "Hosanna! Blessed is the One who comes in the name of the

Lord! Blessed is the coming kingdom of our ancestors! Hosanna in the highest heaven!"

I'm the only person in a throng of thousands who doesn't bow. "I don't understand," I say. "What's happening? What does this mean?"

"Bow," Jude says to me nervously, his face planted flat against the ground. "Bow before the others see you standing!"

I drop to my knees and lay my face in the dirt. "What's happening?"

It's Petra who answers me. "The people know their Scripture."

Miles laughs wildly, his face pressed against the ground. "We were wrong. We were all wrong!"

"About what?" I say, frustrated. "I don't know what you're talking about!"

Petra stands, and we follow his lead, looking ahead at the Teacher, who's now hundreds of yards in front of us. "He's finally answering us." Petra takes a huge gulp of air and tries to calm himself. Then, with a thousand-watt smile, he declares, "He intends to be our warrior king, our messiah of liberation."

"But…how do you know?"

"Prophecy," Miles says. "It's a fulfillment of the Scripture. The prophet Zechariah said, 'Rejoice greatly, O Holy City! See, your king comes to you, righteous and victorious, lowly and riding on a colt. He will take away the chariots and the warhorses from the Holy City, and the battle bow will be broken. He will proclaim peace to the nations. His rule will extend from sea to sea and to the ends of the earth.'"

A chill envelops my body as I understand; we're playing witness to a virgin chapter of history. The messiah will lay siege to the Holy City…in peace.

We run to catch up with the Teacher's impromptu parade, reaching them as they pass through the city gates and enter the holiest and most dangerous city on earth. We've now arrived at the point of no return. The Teacher triumphantly has entered the city, openly receiving the calls of our people, who cry out, "Deliver us! Free us, oh, messiah! Carry us home!"

The Kingdom won't stand for this. To openly identify oneself as the messiah is a crime punishable by death. The trouble officially has begun.

Just inside the gates a new commotion breaks out. I've just noticed the conspicuous absence of centurions when a child screams, "King Charles! It's

King Charles! He's come to the Holy City! Praise God forevermore! Our king comes to bless the people!"

The child's announcement sends an already excited crowd into an electric frenzy. Many, but not all, drop their palm branches and run feverishly in the direction of the child, who leads them away. "Let us bow before our true king!" they scream. "Let us pay tribute to the venerable King Charles, the only son of God!"

And like that, the magic of the Teacher's reverie is broken, the energy crashing as quickly as it was built. "Pathetic," I mutter to Jude. "These people make me sick, their eagerness to grovel before the Kingdom."

"I told you from the start," Jude says, "these poets and dreamers aren't made for war. They cut and run at the first sign of trouble. Not a spine in a single one of them."

"When do we go see the men? Are they in position?"

"Yes. They await our signal in the hills, high above the city walls. We'll meet Henrik tonight and finalize our plans."

"Good. And then I'll go to Maria. She should be here by now."

"Fine, but for the afternoon, we must stay close with the Teacher and track his every move."

"Speaking of," I say, looking around, "where'd he go?"

"To the temple!" someone answers me, rushing by. "The Teacher has gone to the Holy Temple for prayer."

I haven't been to the Holy Temple since I left for school. A magnificent cathedral of white stone and marble, it's the holiest site of our religion, the place where we meet God directly and have our sins forgiven. My parents brought me every year for the Great Festival. We came for the purity rituals, to offer sacrifices, and to celebrate. These memories are some of the fondest of my life.

I remember the first time I saw this place: the enormous columns that seemed to reach all the way to heaven, the brilliantly colored frescos, and the altar table that looked as heavy as the earth itself. All of it felt so sacred and real to me, and I gave thanks to God for his grace—for providing such a place to worship. Approaching this sacred space now brings all these memories back into my heart. I've sorely missed standing upon holy ground.

We hear it before we see it. If I were to live another thousand years and receive a thousand opportunities to predict what happens next, I never would get it right.

Not in a thousand years. Not ever. Not once.

Inside the heavy iron doors of the temple are the moneychangers, the men who sell animals for sacrifice. They've set up tables around the temple, offering their goods to any man with enough money for purchase. In the middle of these men stands the Teacher.

He's screaming at the top of his lungs, flipping over the moneychanger's tables. He's irate. His eyes burn with anger, his face as flushed as a man who hasn't breathed in more than a minute. He storms around the temple, kicking at the tables and tossing buckets of money, driving out any man doing business in this sacred place. The religious authorities holler at him, ordering for him to stop the madness, but the Teacher pays them no mind.

He wrecks the place, thrashing about until every table is destroyed. He cries, "Is it not written, 'My house shall be called a house of prayer for all the nations'? But you have made it a den of robbers! You thieves!"

He keeps teaching this way—*angrily*—for another hour. I expect the religious authorities to attack him at any moment and shut him up. I've never seen anything so outlandish in my life. Here I am—prepared to murder King Charles—and I can't believe what this man is doing.

But they don't arrest him. Then I realize what's happening.

"They're afraid of him," I say to Jude. "They fear us as well. His following has reached a critical mass. They won't move on him."

"The religious authorities won't let this go unpunished," Jude says, picking at the skin on his small hands, looking completely unbothered by what's happening. "They won't allow this sacrilege during the Great Festival."

Annoyed, I leave Jude and move about the frenzied scene, angling myself as close to the religious authorities as possible. I confirm Jude's suspicion. They want the Teacher dead, and they're prepared to petition the Kingdom in order to get it done. One of them, a man with a gray beard who looks like the leader, says, "We can't allow this fraud to disrupt the Great Festival. With King Charles in the Holy City, there will be harsh penalties if our people don't behave. Something must be done about this—and now. We can't afford to wait.

King Charles will have the temple shut down, and the Great Festival will be ruined. Then we'll have to answer to God for the malaise."

I slink away from the religious authorities and draw close again to the Teacher, who continues to teach amid the rubble he's created. As usual the crowd is spellbound, seemingly unaware or without care that the Teacher has made a mess of their sacred temple.

The Teacher looks as tired as ever. As soon as I return to listening to him, he finishes and motions that the time has come to depart. On our way out, Gray Beard, says, "By what authority are you doing these things?"

The Teacher stops walking, turns, and says, "I'll ask you one question. Answer me, and I'll tell you by what authority I do these things." Gray Beard nods. "Did the ministry of the Baptist, my mentor, come from heaven, or was it of human origin? Answer me."

The religious authorities huddle among themselves and argue with one another, saying, "If we say, 'From heaven,' he will say, 'Why then did you not believe him?'"

"Why are they afraid to say 'of human origin'?" I ask Jude.

"Because they know the Baptist was a prophet and their governor had him killed."

Finally Gray Beard says, "We don't know."

The Teacher grins before calmly walking over to the lone chair still standing upright and kicks it hard. The chair screeches wildly across the marble floor, careening to the feet of the religious authorities, who jump out of the way. "Then neither will I tell you by what authority I am doing these things." With that he exits the temple.

This gives me a knot in my stomach, and I tell Jude, "We'd better move quickly, before he gets us all killed."

Outside the Holy Temple, we discover the Teacher isn't ready to call it a day.

"Lord have mercy," Jude says. "We'll all die tonight if he keeps this madness up."

"Shut up, Jude," Petra orders. "The Teacher knows what he's doing. We must trust him, now more than ever. Don't be such a coward."

The people who departed to pay tribute to King Charles have returned. The destruction of the temple has created fresh buzz over the Teacher and his presence in the Holy City. The students help him climb atop a granite obelisk where he addresses the newly invigorated crowd. "I have one more story for the evening," he says. "Let those with ears listen."

The crowd falls quiet, save for one lone voice that cries out, "Give us truth, Teacher! We've come for salvation! Show us the way to God!"

"A man planted a vineyard," the Teacher begins, "put a fence around it, dug a pit for the wine press, and built a watchtower. Then he leased it to tenants and went to another country. When the season came, he sent a slave to the tenants to collect his share of the produce of the vineyard. But they seized him and beat him and sent him away empty-handed." The people hiss in response. The Teacher shrugs. "He sent another slave to them. This one they beat over the head and insulted." The crowd boos and hisses even louder. "Then he sent another, and that one they killed. So it was with many others; some they beat, and others they killed. He had one man left, a beloved son."

A little girl sitting near the Teacher calls out, "Did he send his son to the tenants?"

The Teacher smiles for the first time since he sat atop the colt. "Yes, for he thought the tenants would respect his son."

"Did they?" the child asks.

The Teacher says, "The tenants said to one another, 'This is the heir. Come. Let us kill him, and the inheritance will be ours.' So they seized him, killed him, and threw him out of the vineyard."

The girl jumps to her feet in protest. "What will the owner of the vineyard do?"

Looking directly at the religious authorities, the Teacher says, "He'll come and destroy the tenants and give the vineyard to others. Have you not read this scripture: 'The stone that the builders rejected has become the cornerstone; this was the Lord's doing, and it is amazing in our eyes'?"

Again the religious authorities explode in anger, understanding fully that the Teacher is speaking against them. Many of them openly discuss stoning him right here and right now, but Gray Beard knows better. "Should we kill him, the people will revolt against us, and we'll all be dead." Then, breaking away from his own, he approaches the Teacher and says, "Young teacher, I see you're sincere and show deference to no one, for you don't regard people with partiality but teach the way of God in accordance with truth. Tell us then, is it lawful for our people to pay taxes to King Charles?"

"Why are you putting me to this test?" the Teacher asks. He waits for an answer, but one doesn't come. "Never mind. Bring me a World coin, and let me see it."

I reach for a coin in my own pocket and toss it to the Teacher. Catching it in his hand, he says, "Whose head is this on the coin? Who is this man?"

"King Charles," I answer loudly for all to hear.

Miles, who stands near me, says, "This is it—he's going to whip up a rebellion. Get ready, boys. Our time has come!"

The Teacher lifts the coin high in the air and turns himself in a full circle, regarding the crowd who's come to listen. "Give to the king the things that are his...and give to God the things that are God's."

"What?" Petra says, breathless and crestfallen. "No...what is he saying?"

A discontented murmur shoots through the crowd. Sensing a turn in the momentum, Gray Beard says, "One more question, Teacher! Which commandment in Scripture is the first of all?"

Without skipping a beat, the Teacher says, "The first is, 'Hear, O People: The Lord our God, the Lord is one; you shall love the Lord your God with all your heart, and with all your soul, and with all your mind, and with all your strength.' The second is this, 'You shall love your neighbor as yourself.' There is no other commandment greater than these."

After that no one dares ask the Teacher any more questions.

I don't even care, because the Teacher's words have struck a chord deep within me. It was this teaching, "To love others as we love ourselves," that stole my love from me. Maria believes this supposedly wise virtue, and because of it, she left me to care for Alejandro.

And here I find myself...in the Holy City, on the brink of a war, alone.

I blame no one but the Teacher for it.

# CHAPTER 23

We meet Henrik beneath the cover of darkness. The Holy City is a marvelously intricate metropolis with hundreds of high-rises, diverse neighborhoods, and plenty of dark alleys where men can meet for stealthy conversation—even when the city is filled to capacity, as it is now.

This is the first time Henrik and I have been face-to-face since I nearly killed him. I should fear this man who stands nearly two feet taller than I do—but I don't.

I can't.

I'm convinced Henrik had something to do with my parents' abduction into the camps, and for that I'll hate the man until I see life snuffed from his eyes. Even then I'll pray for the torment of his soul.

But for now, in this moment, Henrik is of vital importance to my cause, which means I have no choice but to tolerate him. I would partner with the Evil One himself if it meant killing King Charles.

Under the darkness it's difficult to get a good read on Henrik's face, but I see enough to realize it's still severely bruised and swollen. "Hello, Henrik," I say casually, a little grin running off my face.

Henrik grunts and tells Jude, "You'd better get your man under control."

"Yes, Deacon. I believe you have something you wanted to say to Henrik. Isn't that right?"

"No," I say. "Don't believe I do."

"Deacon," Jude says sternly, "apologize to Henrik. Now."

"The only thing I'm sorry for is not killing you when I had the chance."

Henrik takes a step closer to me. "I wonder if you'll change your tune when I'm the only one standing between you and the wrath of King Charles's army," he says.

"What are you talking about?"

Henrik laughs darkly. "Jude hasn't explained it to you yet?"

"Explained what?"

Jude steps in. "Both of you need to take a breath."

"Explain what, Jude?" I say.

Jude clears his throat. "I won't be with you when you meet King Charles."

"Why not?"

"Because," Henrik says, "he'll be in the hills with the army."

"I thought one of your men was going to lead the charge into the city."

"That was the plan," Jude says timidly, "but the men are growing restless. They've been under the leadership of Henrik's men for some time, and Henrik thinks morale will be boosted if I go to them *before* the charge."

"A few weeks ago, those men were ready to storm the gates of hell," I say. "When I left they would have followed me off a cliff. What happened?"

"Yes," Jude says, "and when they see you take off King Charles's head, they'll be reignited with that same passion. But Henrik is right. I should go to them and lead the charge myself."

I don't like this. The plan is already risky enough. If I'm going to kill King Charles in broad daylight, with an army of centurions surrounding the city, I want at least one fellow rebel by my side. I don't want to do this alone.

"Our odds of survival were slim enough with three of us on the palace landing," I say. "How do you envision the two of us surviving until our army breaches the city? Once I kill the king, what's going to stop the other centurions from killing me?"

"You have to remember," Jude says, "at the ceremony, King Charles will be accompanied by only two body guards, one of which is Henrik. You kill the king. Henrik takes out the other centurion, and then all hell breaks loose in the city. By the time the commanders of the Centurion Guard realize what's happening, our army will be charging into the city, laying waste to everything in our path." Jude issues a nervous breath. "On its face the plan sounds crazy, but in actuality it's not that risky. The Gratitude Ceremony is the only time when King Charles is so ill protected, so exposed."

Henrik adds, "Tradition dictates the king display true humility when thanking the families."

"And surrounding oneself with centurions who executed their family isn't exactly the best way to do that?"

"Bingo," Jude says.

I look at Henrik, and everything about him feels wrong. "So," I say, "I'm supposed to trust you with my life?"

"No," he says. "You're supposed to kill the king and trust it'll be enough to galvanize your army to lead a successful insurrection."

"And you've been paid...with my money?"

"All our debts have been paid," Jude answers for Henrik.

"Is that all this is about for you, Henrik? Money?"

Henrik ignores me and says to Jude, "We're working with the religious authorities, so I'll have to confirm, but we'll most likely take the Teacher on Thursday. Be ready."

"We will," Jude says.

With that the man I've wanted to kill for years disappears into a hot and dishonest night.

I once thought there was no worse fate than to grieve for my parents alone. But I was wrong. It's infinitely worse to partner with the man who dug their graves. To avenge my parents' deaths, it turns out, means I must betray them first.

# CHAPTER 24

I roam the city all night in search of Maria.

I don't find her.

At daybreak I return to the temple and find the Teacher hard at work, as he always is. I locate Petra and the others and take my place among them. The Teacher once again has aimed his criticism not at the Kingdom but at our own religious authorities—an action that increasingly grates on my nerves. I can't understand why he spends so much time arguing with *them* instead of aiming his wrath at the true enemy—the Kingdom.

"Beware of the scribes," he says, "who like to walk around in long robes, and to be greeted with respect in the marketplaces, and to have the best seats in the temple and places of honor at banquets! They devour widows' houses and, for the sake of appearance, say long prayers. They'll receive the greater condemnation."

As the Teacher speaks, Southerners approach the temple in droves to deposit their taxes into the Kingdom treasury, which has been strategically placed at the temple, since all Southerners will visit the temple during the Great Festival. It's just one example of how the Kingdom desecrates our religion.

A poor widow appears in the midst of those paying taxes and deposits two small copper coins, which are worth practically nothing. Seeing this the Teacher calls our attention to her and says, "Truly I tell you, this poor widow has put in more than all those who are contributing to the treasury. They have contributed out of their abundance, but she, out of her poverty, has put in everything she had, all she had to live on."

That does it. I can't stand it anymore and am shouting before I realize what I'm saying. "And this is a good thing?" I call out to the Teacher. "That a poor widow gives away her last pennies? Did I hear you right?"

Jude elbows me in the rib cage. "What are you doing? Shut your mouth!"

"I'm sorry," I say, loud enough for everyone to hear. "I can't listen to this any longer! Here we are, in the Holy City, with the Kingdom breathing down our backs, stealing our money, and all you do is talk about our own religion! *What about them?* What about the murderous centurions who rob our very way of life? What have you to say to them, oh, wise Teacher?"

The Teacher moves toward me, the people parting like the Red Sea before him. Pointing at the skyline of the Holy City, he says, "Do you see these great buildings, Deacon? Do you see these magnificent buildings?"

I'm red hot with anger. "Yes," I say. "I see them."

"Not one stone will be left here upon another; all will be thrown down."

"When? Tell me…when will this happen?"

"When you hear of wars and rumors of wars, don't be alarmed. This must take place, but the end is still to come, for nation will rise against nation and kingdom against kingdom. There will be earthquakes and famines. This is but the beginning of the birth pangs."

"You know what I think?" My voice cracks under the strain of anger. "I think you're afraid to do what must be done."

"Deacon," Jude says, taking my arm firmly in his hands, "you need to watch your mouth."

After a long moment, the Teacher says the following words as carefully and sincerely as I've heard him say anything during my time with him. "But the good news must first be proclaimed to the nations, Deacon."

"How can there be good news while we groan under the tyranny of the Kingdom?" My anger breaks as I say these words and is displaced with sorrow; grief floods my soul. "Please, Teacher, I need to know. I…must…understand the way."

The Teacher cups my face in his hands, and I let him do it. His hands are sweaty and calloused, but the way he holds me—it makes me feel as safe as a child with his father.

*Safety*—an emotion I haven't felt since my parents were taken.

The Teacher holds my head perfectly still for several long moments and looks with care into my eyes. Then, staring only at me, says, "You will be hated by all…because of my name. But the one who endures to the end will be saved. Will you endure for me, Deacon? Will you?"

I try to answer him, but I can't, because I'm once again weeping with the Teacher.

# CHAPTER 25

I t's the eve before the Great Festival, and I've abandoned everyone. I've
spent the past few days on my own, searching for Maria.

Because...I can't go through with it.

I can't betray the Teacher. To be honest, I don't think I can explain my decision. My head is the foggiest it's ever been. I am ages beyond the clear-headed
vision of my train ride home when I knew precisely who I was and what I was
going to do.

Revenge. That's all I've lived for, and all I've wanted. Kill those who took my
parents, and keep killing until they killed me. That was my plan, plain and simple.
Take as many of them to the grave as humanly possible. Then die the death of a
warrior. Die gloriously on the battlefield and join my parents in the afterlife.

But the Teacher has done something to me. My soul has been stirred so
deeply that I believe it has awakened, perhaps for the first time in my life. But
that's not really true. Maria woke up my soul first, but...this is different. It has
me thinking confused and troubling thoughts, which isn't good, because I need
to be focused or it'll all fall apart. Maybe it already has.

So I vanished. I said nothing to Miles and Petra. Then I abandoned Jude,
who's probably having a nervous breakdown right now.

I don't care; I had to do it. Nothing matters to me anymore except finding
Maria. All I want is to find her and escape this city. To hell with the rebellion.

I've scoured every nook of the Holy City and found no trace of her, not
the faintest hint of her lavender perfume. I've been to every temple, hotel, café,
and bar. I've hounded strangers on the street. Last night I was nearly arrested
by the Centurion Guard for public belligerence.

I'm losing my mind. I'm not the true messiah; I can't be, because that title
belongs to someone else. This epiphany both confounds me and brings me the

greatest comfort I've known. Because if it's true, then the true messiah will do what must be done. Which means I'm free to love and be loved in return— something I'm finally ready to do.

If only I can find Maria.

It's late now, and the streets are thin as people head home to prepare for the festival. I'm so exhausted that I slump down on the corner of a dimly lit street. The pavement is wet from a light but hot evening shower. I've just eaten a heavy meal of pasta and drunk far too much white wine. I lie back against the wet concrete, and the buildings above my head spin wildly. I close my eyes and hope to pass out quickly.

That's when I hear her laugh—the one I would recognize from the grave. My eyes pop open, and I spring to my feet.

She laughs again.

There! At the end of the street, I see a woman tossing back black hair. Then she disappears into a building, followed closely by a giant. I slip and fall on the wet concrete, landing hard on my aching wrist. Cursing, I climb back to my feet and continue to run, my arm throbbing with pain, my stomach nauseous. "Maria!" I scream. "Wait! Maria! Wait!"

But she's already gone. At the end of the street, I lunge for the door she disappeared through and fling it open. The doorway leads into a small stairwell that takes me down several floors beneath the street's surface. At the bottom I find another door, but it's locked.

I bang furiously on the thick wood, crying out Maria's name. It doesn't open. I bang harder and louder, my voice reaching a crescendo of fury and urgency.

It still doesn't open.

I pull my gun and prepare to shoot through the door.

The lock turns, and the door inches open. "Who's there?" comes a hostile voice.

"Maria?" I slur. "It's me, Deacon! Maria!"

"Deacon?" the voice says. "Where on earth have you been?" The door swings wide, and Miles welcomes me into the room. I stow the gun in my waistband and stumble into the cramped chamber, ignoring him as he tries to hug me.

They're all here. The Teacher. The students. An angry Jude. Even Alejandro sits furtively in the corner of the room, avoiding eye contact with me. In this small room, he appears even larger, like an adult sitting in a child's make-believe house. There's another face in the group, one I immediately recognize. It's the scarred face of the leper whom the Teacher healed the first night I met him in the park.

All of them are seated at a U-shaped table.

All of them but Maria, that is. I feverishly scan the room but don't see her. I look again, inspecting each face carefully, but she's nowhere to be found. "Where is she?" I ask.

Only the leper speaks to me. "Welcome to my home. May I offer you some water? You look thirsty."

"Where's Maria?"

Then she appears, standing before the Teacher, a dripping sponge in her hands. She's even more gorgeous than I remembered her in my dreams. She tilts her toward me but doesn't smile.

She's crying; thick tears smear heavy makeup I've never seen her wear. She's dressed in a simple but elegant white gown and is done up as if she were getting married. Her face, however, couldn't be further from that of a blushing bride; it's the longest, saddest face in the world.

I rush to her side, clumsily stumbling past the others. I failed Maria the last time she stood before me. I treated her as a little boy might and not a man. I won't make the same mistake twice.

"Maria," I say, wrapping my arms tightly around her. "My Maria," I whisper into her ear. "You came. You came to the Holy City."

A warm, thick liquid drips from her sponge, wetting my clothes. She says, "I thought something happened to you. I thought you did something—something foolish—and the Kingdom snatched you away."

"Never," I say. "They'll never take me away from you. Where have you been?" I'm fully aware that every man in the room, including the Teacher, is listening to our conversation, but I don't care. All that matters is that Maria is here and knows of my love, my loyalty to her.

"Here," Maria replies, as if her answer were the most obvious thing in the world. "I've been here with the Teacher and my brothers. Where else would I be?" She wipes her face. "We've been looking for you."

My eyes dart to Alejandro then back to her.

"No," she says decisively, reading my mind. That does it for me. Nothing more needs to be said of him. Maria is mine.

"I've been looking for you," I say. "I was terrified the Kingdom kidnapped you in Oxford."

"Why would the Kingdom kidnap me?"

I start to answer then think better of it. "Forget it. All that matters is you're safe."

"We need to talk," Maria says, "but first there's something I must do." She releases me and drops to her knees before the Teacher. She takes his head in her hands and tilts him forward. He gives himself to her. Then she takes the sponge, dips it into a jar of oil sitting on the floor, and begins to wash his head. She works her fingers slowly from the crown outward, methodically working the oil into every pore of his scalp.

The Teacher groans and breathes out deeply in satisfaction. I suddenly feel as though my eyes are trespassing onto sacred ground. I look at the other men. They appear tense and confused.

"What are you doing?" I ask Maria.

"Shut up!" Petra orders. "Take a seat, Deacon, and be quiet."

"I don't understand. What's happening?"

Miles stands up, takes me by the shoulder, and leads me to a seat at the table. I'm too tired and tipsy to resist him. I sit in a stunned stupor for what feels like a very long time as Maria anoints the Teacher's head. The sweet scent of the oil wafts through the room, as do the Teacher's sighs and soft cries.

There are rare moments in life of inexplicable beauty, times when you know something significant is happening but you don't understand its power.

This moment is such a time. I don't know what my precious Maria has done, but I know it matters; I know it is of monumental importance for both her and the Teacher who saved her life. I don't understand it, but I'm smart enough to respect it and keep my mouth closed.

Jude slams his fists on the tabletop. "Why was the ointment wasted in this way? That oil is insanely expensive! That jar costs more Worlds than the average American makes in a year. We could have sold that jar and given the money to the poor." Turning to Maria, he adds, "You, *woman*, should be ashamed of yourself for being so wasteful. Surely you must know the Teacher would have preferred the money to be spent elsewhere."

"Leave her alone," the Teacher says in a tender voice. "She has performed a good service for me."

"And why is that?" I say, genuinely curious. "What purpose does this serve?"

The Teacher puts a finger on Maria's chin. "You'll always have the poor with you, and you can show kindness to them whenever you wish, but you won't always have me. She has done what she could. She has anointed my body beforehand for its burial."

The room issues a collective gasp.

"Burial!" Petra exclaims. "What burial? There will be no burial!"

The Teacher leans back in his seat and closes his eyes. "Truly I tell you, wherever the good news is proclaimed in the whole world, what she has done will be told in remembrance of her."

Jude slaps a cup of water and sends it flying across the room. He kicks his chair back and rockets upward. "I've heard enough! Deacon, we're leaving. Let's go."

I don't move. Instead I wait. I wait for Maria to turn and ask me to stay. I wait for her to step away from the Teacher and come to me. I won't force her. I won't even ask. She must choose. I wait.

A second ticks by. Then another. And another. And another.

"Deacon," Jude says, "we need to go—right now."

I stand but make no movement to leave. Time stands still. Finally Maria lifts her head and says, "I love you, Deacon, but if you must go, you must go."

"Come with me," I say, choking on the word. "Come…"

Maria tucks her long her hair behind her ears, walks gracefully across the room, and takes me in her arms. It's the loveliest moment of my life. She squeezes my face tenderly before running her hands around my neck and down the length of my back, scratching delicately until her fingers find the hard ridges of the gun.

She freezes, as if turned to stone. In a confused whisper, she says, "You… promised me."

"I did. I mean, I tried to get rid of it, but something happened. It's what I've been trying to tell you."

"Talk to me, Deacon. Tell me now!" She tries hard to look hopeful, but I can see how deeply hurt she is. I've betrayed her. She knows I wouldn't have left with her that day, even if Alejandro hadn't shown up. She knows I'm a liar.

I glance furtively at the other men in the room. "Are you serious? Here? Maybe we should go outside?"

"I'm not the only person in this room who loves you. We all do. Whatever's going on with you, you can say it here. Let us help you. Let *me* help you. Let the Teacher help you."

Miles interjects, "You're our brother, Deacon. What do you need?"

The door opens behind me, and Jude says, "Now or never, Deacon."

"It's early," I say to Jude. "We still have time."

"But not long," the Teacher says from his seat. "Our hours run late, and the Son of Man will soon be betrayed." He smiles warmly at me. "But Deacon, I'm so happy you've rejoined us. Will you stay for supper?"

I glance back at Jude. "I know where to find you."

"Teacher?" Jude says, disgusted with me. "Will you be in the garden tonight for prayer?"

The corners of the Teacher's mouth sink down. He wants to keep smiling but clearly can't. "I will, and you, my dear Jude, should join me."

Jude exits without another word. I slip my hand into Maria's and take my place at the Teacher's table.

It's the greatest meal of my life. Not the food—the food and wine are simple. It's the community, the experience of sitting at a table with my brothers and the woman I love. It's the knowledge that these people love me, that I'm not alone in this world.

It's the fellowship, the primeval voice whispering that most sacred of truths. People—all people—have a place at the table; we are one. It's the message of the Teacher I'm finally, at last, beginning to understand; no one is excluded from his table. Not even his betrayers. Not even his enemies.

I once heard the Teacher say we should love our enemies and pray for those who persecute us. I didn't understand him then, and I'm not sure I do now, but somehow, in some way, this meal is connected with that teaching. It must be. Otherwise I wouldn't be sitting here.

Maria and I share few words during the meal, but when I put my hand on her knee, she doesn't push it away. Later, when I slide it farther up her leg, she interlocks her fingers with mine.

The Teacher takes bread from the table, lifts it high, and blesses it. Then he breaks it and passes it around the table, saying, "Take; this is my body."

We pass the bread, each of us tearing off a piece and eating it. When this is done, the Teacher raises his glass of wine and says, "This is my blood of the covenant, which is poured out for many." He tips the glass back and drinks deeply from it. Then he says, "Truly I tell you, I never again will drink of the fruit of the vine until that day when I drink it new in the kingdom of God."

We raise our glasses and toast his exciting promise.

"Wait. Before you drink from your own cup," the Teacher says, "drink first from mine." He passes his cup to Petra, who drinks from it and passes it to Miles. Then Miles passes it to Maria, and Maria to me. And around the table it goes.

Each person raises the cup and drinks the wine. When the cup finds its way back to the Teacher, he places it on the table. "Let us sing a hymn to praise the one true God," he says. "Maria, would you be so kind?"

Immediately Maria begins to sing in her raspy, sultry voice.

*The Lord is my light and my salvation*
*Whom then shall I fear?*
*The Lord is the strength of my life.*
*Of whom then shall I be afraid?*

The others join her, but I don't sing. Instead I reflect on the Teacher, who sings with his eyes closed. Until this night I haven't known what to make of him. To be honest, I still don't. But I do know this; he's not the messiah we expected, but I'm beginning to suspect he's the messiah we need. My father used to say our greatness is defined by how we treat the weakest among us. I wonder what my father would have made of this man who refuses to ignore the suffering of those around him. This man who lifts up the downtrodden. This man who breaks bread and drinks wine with his friends *and* his enemies.

*When evildoers came upon me to eat up my flesh,*
*it was they,*
*my foes and my adversaries,*
*who stumbled and fell.*
*Though an army should encamp against me,*
*yet my heart shall not be afraid.*
*And though war should rise up against me,*
*yet will I put my trust in him.*

I'm singing now with the others, praying to God these words may be true in my life. I've been scared for a long time. That's the truth. And only two things have made me feel better—revenge and Maria.

Not prayer. In fact, as the words pour out of my mouth, I realize this is the first time I've prayed since my parents' death. I don't know why that is, but I find it troubling.

*One thing I have asked of the Lord,*
*one thing I seek,*
*that I may dwell in the house of the Lord*
*all the days of my life.*

The song ends, and the Teacher stands. The rest of us follow. The mood of the room has been transformed from when I first stumbled in. Gone is the jilted silence. In its place are joy and the deep satisfaction that only a meal with friends can provide.

Then the Teacher speaks and ruins everything. "You'll all become deserters, for it is written, 'I will strike the shepherd, and the sheep will be scattered.'"

"No," Petra says, waving his hands wildly. "*No*. Even if all of them become deserters, I won't."

"Truly I tell you, this day, this *very* night, before the cock crows twice, you'll deny me three times."

"No, Teacher!" Petra spits vehemently. "Even if I must die with you, I won't deny you." Petra looks around the room for support. "Isn't that right? Tell him, Miles! Maria, tell him! We would never betray you!"

They all agree. Each person pledges his allegiance to the Teacher. They all swear by the one true God that they'd sooner meet death than betray the Teacher.

I wish I could say the same.
I honestly do.
But I can't.
And I won't.

# CHAPTER 26

It's time to meet Jude for the betrayal. The Kingdom has given the religious authorities permission to have him arrested for his disturbance in the temple. The Kingdom cares nothing about our worship, but they do care about keeping peace when thousands of Southerners pour into the Holy City for the Great Festival. A famous holy man destroying this sacred place is an excellent way to incite a riot. The Kingdom no longer can afford to sit back and let the Teacher be free.

His time has come.

But I don't go to Jude. Instead I remain with Maria. I can't stop what I've put into motion; I can only hope Maria will understand why I've done it. This is my last chance to get her to see the situation from my perspective.

After singing the hymn, the Teacher led us quietly through the outskirts of the Holy City and to a hillside where a quiet garden awaited us. He asked us to stay awake and pray for him, and then he left, climbing farther up the hill to pray alone, as is his custom.

Maria and I are now settled together on the ground, far enough from the others that we can speak in private. The garden is supremely quiet, save for Petra's snoring. Even Alejandro rests peacefully on the ground. Everyone is exhausted from the long days of travel and the frenzied pace of ministering to thousands.

Maria's skin once again touching mine is a pleasure so divine that it should be reserved for the afterlife. This night reminds me of our first night in the park; only this time our bond is infinitely more intense. She notices me favoring my bandaged wrist and says, "Your whole body is busted. How did this happen?"

"Doesn't matter." I stroke her face with my good hand. "I thought I might never be with you again."

"Where did you go, Deacon, the night before Alejandro returned? Why did you leave me?"

I tell Maria everything.

Almost.

The gun…Jude…the army…even my epic fight with Henrik. I relish every detail of my triumph over him, desperate to impress upon Maria that I'm a man fit to lead. Then, finally, *slowly*, I tell her what the men called me: "messiah."

"But how can this be?" she says. "The Teacher is the messiah."

"That's just it, my love. I used to believe there was only one way to freedom, but now I see I was wrong. The way of the Teacher is true and righteous, but…"

"But what?"

"But there are different roles for us all to play. He uses words; I use might. He gives the people a blessing; I give them weapons. Both are important."

"Deacon, this isn't the way. The Teacher says we must turn the other cheek and return evil with love. He has done away with 'An eye for an eye and a tooth for a tooth.' You've heard his teachings, just as I have. The new age will be forged in love, not hatred. You must stop hating your enemies if you're ever to love them. Violence will only beget more violence. Don't you see? It's a vicious cycle that will never end unless we stop it ourselves."

"I don't want to love my enemies, Maria. It's absurd. I want to kill my enemies before they kill me. I want to eradicate the Kingdom before every last one of our people has been hauled off to the north in a death train."

Maria and I stare at each other until she understands how serious I am. Then, with great pain in her voice, says, "When is this army of yours planning to attack?"

I check to make sure the others are still sleeping. Petra's loud snoring confirms it. "Tomorrow," I say in a hushed voice. "In the morning."

"On the day of the Great Festival! How could you, Deacon? It's the holiest day of the year. God will never forgive it."

"*Shh!* Maria, lower your voice." I check again to see if our voices have awoken anyone. "Forgive it?" I whisper. "God demands it!"

Before she can answer, the Teacher stumbles down the hill, calling to us, "Have you all fallen asleep?" His voice is tortured, a toxic blend of anger and stress. He trips and falls to the ground.

Maria runs to him. "Teacher!" she cries out.

This wakes Petra and the others from their slumber.

"I came twice before," the Teacher says heavily, "and saw that you all were sleeping."

"Teacher," Maria says, taking his head in her arms, "what's wrong?"

"I'm deeply grieved," he says. "I need you—all of you—to remain awake and pray."

"We will, Teacher!" Petra says groggily, putting the heels of his hands to his eyes. "We will pray with you. You can count on us."

"Petra, could you not keep awake one single hour?" the Teacher says. "Keep awake, and pray that you may not come into the time of trial. The spirit indeed is willing, but the flesh is weak." The Teacher stands and walks awkwardly back up the hill. He falls again after only a few yards. Driving his hands into the dirt, he lifts his head to the starry night sky and cries out, "Father! Father! For you all things are possible. Remove this cup from me—yet not what I want but what you want."

He drops his head like a powerless infant and continues to pray, this time in silence.

Then it happens. The moment I've been dreading and anticipating.

In the distance...movement. Rustling. Voices. Dark voices. Boots shuffling. Guns bolting. Heat rising.

Petra calls out into the darkness. "Who's there?"

The darkness offers no reply. A falling star streaks madly across the sky, as if delivering an urgent celestial message.

The Teacher speaks first. Rising meekly from the ground, he says, "Enough! The hour has come. The Son of Man has been betrayed into the hands of sinners." Then, looking directly at me, he says, "Get up. Let's get going. My betrayer is at hand."

# CHAPTER 27

Jude leads the religious authorities, and the armed guards who've accompanied them, to the Teacher. The angry mob halts their progress roughly twenty yards from the rest of us.

Only Jude continues to walk. The religious authorities stand still, surrounded by men with guns. Jude approaches me first. In a voice I've come to distrust, he says, "You've done your very best to ruin this week. You've done everything in your power to destroy what your father prepared." He puts a hand behind his back. "I pray to the gods it's all out of your system. This is your time, Deacon." He pokes my chest with his thin finger but keeps his other hand behind his back. "Time to wake up and look fate in the eye. Embrace the role your people have given you." He slaps my cheek entirely too hard. "May the God who formed you have mercy on your soul, should you fail to do his bidding, should you dare to reject the call of the anointed one."

Petra charges toward Jude like a raging bull, hell-bent on a bloody goring. Miles follows closely behind. "What is this? What's going on? Jude, why have you brought these fools here?"

I see a bulge underneath Petra's shirt. I don't know where he got it, but he has a weapon.

Jude ignores Petra and walks toward the Teacher, who's standing next to Maria. The Teacher looks as though he's just received the worst news of his life.

Petra raises his voice. "I'm talking to you!"

"Petra," I say thinly. "It's…all right. Let them be."

Petra explodes. "*Let them be? Let them be?* Jude has brought these vermin into our camp, and you want to let them be? Have you lost your nerve, Deacon?"

"They're armed," I say. "You need to be careful. These men are incredibly dangerous."

"Is that right?" Petra says.

"It is," Miles agrees. "Listen to Deacon, Petra. Take a deep breath, old friend. I sense great danger tonight."

"Good," Petra says. "Because I'm also a dangerous man. And it's about damn time somebody knew it."

Petra marches toward the Teacher, and Miles tries to stop him. Petra grabs his old friend by the neck and shoves him to the ground. Wounded, Miles timidly extends a hand up to me, but I leave him where he lies.

I sprint across the garden to find Jude and the Teacher standing face-to-face. Petra hovers directly behind Jude. The Teacher orders Petra to stay where he is. Petra is hot, but he obeys. He's like a hunting dog, desperate to spring for the chase.

No one moves. The men with guns keep their weapons pointed at the dirt.

I know the signal, and I'm aware it's about to happen, yet I can't bring myself to either condone or stop it. I'm as conflicted as a nation at civil war; I'm my own brother and my own enemy. I'm a soul divided and somehow already conquered.

Petra points to the religious authorities. "I'll kill any man who lays a finger on the Teacher."

"Teacher," Jude says.

"Good evening, Jude."

And there it is.

Jude kisses his teacher.

The tenderness on the Teacher's face will haunt me for the rest of my days. Here, in the moment of betrayal, he continues to love his students—even those of us who've become his enemies.

The men with guns move very fast. Three of them close the gap with vicious speed. They seize the Teacher, bind his hands, and strike him across the face. Jude is pushed roughly aside. Petra pulls a knife from his waistband and lunges at one of the armed men. He cuts off his ear before a gun is shoved in his face. The man with the missing ear shrieks in pain. A thick chunk of flesh falls to the ground. Blood spews from the side of his head.

A melee ensues. Fists fly. Boots stomp. Miles takes a hard shot to his chin and goes down. After that I don't see what happens to him. I dart straight for

Maria. I don't know if these men know who I am, but I'm not about to risk an arrest.

I snatch Maria before anyone else can and push her from the tangle of men. As we retreat from the fray, Alejandro roars to life. He storms past me, the dark fire returned to his eyes, and barrels over one of the guards, grabbing him by the throat and breaking his neck. Then, with the agility of a jungle cat, he bounds into the woods and ascends a tree. Before he disappears into the darkness, however, he stops and turns his head back toward me, a full ninety degrees. His eyes are dark-red embers. He opens his mouth and unfurls his tongue. It drops a full foot beneath his chin. With a hiss he launches himself off the tree into a thicket of branches and disappears. A cold wind whips spitefully through the garden.

A single shot rings out loudly above our heads, and the melee grinds to a halt.

It's the Teacher who brings order to the chaos, saying, "Petra! Put down your weapon." Blood drips from the Teacher's nose and runs into his mouth when speaks. His cheek is swollen. He cranes his heads toward the religious authorities, who stand safely behind the wall of their armed guards, and says, "Have you come out with guns to arrest me, as though I were a criminal, some kind of bandit? Day after day I was with you in the temple teaching and you didn't arrest me. But let the scriptures be fulfilled."

Petra's face says it all. It's as though every hope and dream he's ever had has been dashed against the rocks. He's a man watching his house burn to the ground. He looks crestfallen, totally dejected. The Teacher isn't the messiah Petra desperately hoped he would be. The mighty warrior is supposed to cut off King Charles's head, not allow a few old men drag him away into night.

In this sense I feel Jude and I have done the other students a favor. We're exposing the Teacher for who he is. He's a great and peaceful holy man—make no mistake about it. He works miracles. He gives hope to the downtrodden.

But he isn't a messiah. He won't—and can't—deliver the people from their bondage.

Only I can do that.

A guard punches Petra in the stomach, and he drops the knife as he falls to his knees. The armed men laugh. Fat Belly and Gray Beard slap each other on the back. They're delighted as schoolboys on the first evening of summer.

Maria panics as we flee the garden for the darkness of the surrounding woods. I guide her hurriedly, and we both trip and stumble over hallowed logs and knotty roots. In tears she says, "Where have they gone?"

"I don't know. Don't worry; they won't hurt him. They promised me."

"Not the Teacher," she says, catching herself on a tree stump.

"Who?"

"My brothers!"

I stop running and peer back into the garden. I can't believe my eyes.

As the guards drag the Teacher away from the garden and toward the Holy City, not a single student, other than Petra, remains.

All of them, in this dark hour, have abandoned the Teacher.

# CHAPTER 28

Maria thrashes against my chest, begging for me to let her go. She wants to chase after the guards, to go and find where they're taking the Teacher. She swears she'll never forgive me if I let something happen to him.

Nothing I say can make it better. But I won't release her.

Petra picks himself up from the ground, and Maria calls to him as I drag her away. "Follow them, Petra!" she says. "Don't let them hurt him!"

Petra points at me. "You did this, didn't you? I'll kill you, Deacon—you and Jude!" Then he turns and runs off into the night. Petra is the only student—other than Maria—brave enough to follow the Teacher toward danger.

Maria's tears dry up.

"Did you?" she says. Her voice is cold as ice water.

"Did I what?" I say, leading her back into the garden, where I kneel to pick up Petra's knife. It's a switchblade, and I have no clue where he got it. I fold the blade into the sheath and slide the knife beneath the bandage on my sprained wrist. Two weapons are better than one.

"Deacon! Did you? Answer me!"

"What?" I repeat. As we walk, I keep my eyes peeled wide for Alejandro. He's still in these woods, watching us. I can feel it. His demons have returned. Legion is back.

"What Petra said!" Maria cries. "Did you have something to do with this? Did you tell them where we were?"

I know better than to immediately answer her. I decisively lead her farther into the woods. Finally, when I'm certain of what I want to say, and certain she'd be lost without me, I speak. "Don't you see, Maria? Look back into the garden. Where is everyone? Where have all the students gone? It's just you and me."

"I don't know, and I don't care."

"These men aren't made to fight," I say. "And that's OK. Neither is the Teacher."

We duck under a low branch.

"Did you betray him?"

"Maria…"

"Answer me. Now."

She teeters on the edge; our relationship hangs in the balance. One wrong move and this woman, who's as loyal as the moon, will be gone. A deep current runs in her, and I know that if she decides to leave me, I won't be able to stop her. If she believes I've conspired against the Teacher, she'll leave me no matter what.

"I allowed this to happen for his protection."

Maria slaps me hard across the face.

It stings, but I try not to show it. Tears well in the corners of my eyes. I stand firmly at attention, staring straight into her black eyes.

She does it again.

I flex my jaw, grimace, and absorb the pain. It feels like a match lit against my cheek. She's a surprisingly strong woman. My pain is made much worse by the fact that my face is already bruised from the beatings I've taken this past week.

A long moment passes between us.

Finally she says, "I'm sorry. I shouldn't have done that. I shouldn't hit you. I shouldn't strike anyone."

"No…it's all right. I deserve it."

Maria pulls her hair from her face and wipes her eyes.

"The religious authorities want him dead," I say matter-of-factly. "The spectacle at the temple was too much. He's broken nearly every law in their book. They weren't going to allow it for much longer. I know this is difficult for you to understand, but the best way to protect the Teacher was to hand him over. Were he to continue preaching tomorrow, they could have gone to the Kingdom and demanded his arrest for being a rebel. Do you have any idea what would happen if they charged him with that?"

Maria nods sharply.

"But do you really?" I say.

"Yes."

"Tell me. I want you to say the words."

"The cross."

"That's right." I take her teary face in the palms of my hands. "They'd hang him on a Kingdom cross. Is that what you want? For your beloved Teacher to die from the cruelest form of death ever devised?"

"Of course not. But what makes you think they won't hurt him tonight?"

"It's the eve of the Great Festival. To try him tonight would violate our religious laws. There can be no trial until sunrise. But that will never happen. They're going to lock him up until the Great Festival is over. Can you imagine the scandal of a midnight trial of the Teacher? The people would stone the religious authorities for such an atrocity. Nothing will happen tonight, I swear it."

"And then what?"

"It doesn't matter."

"Why not?"

"Because tomorrow night, when all this is over, you and I will find the Teacher and walk straight out of the Holy City—together—with an army behind us."

"No. They're never going to let him go. When the festival is over, they'll torture him."

"No they won't," I tell her.

"How can you be so sure?"

"Because," I say, my chest welling with pride, "they won't be able to."

"Why not?"

"They'll be dead."

# CHAPTER 29

Maria hates the plan.

She says I'm risking my very soul by waging war during the Great Festival—not to mention the fact that I plan on killing holy men. No matter how noble the cause, the ends—she argues—don't justify the means.

She's wrong. But I understand she can't see that tonight. It's far too late, and there's still far too much for me to do. But when the dust settles, and this city's streets are flooded with the blood of our enemies, she'll see the light.

I drop her off at the safe house Henrik has prepared for us. It's a cramped apartment on the top floor of a formidable high-rise. Built twenty years ago, the building is half filled with occupants. The apartment has running water, canned food, and a twin bed I'm told is comfortable for sleeping. The high-rise is situated miles from where the battle will take place. It's as safe a hideout as can be within Holy City limits. Henrik has assured us that most of the occupants are Kingdom citizens, meaning the building will be fortified should things run sideways. But I've already planned for that. My men are aware that Maria will be here and will keep this in mind when the fighting heats up. Under no circumstances will this building be attacked.

I feel good about leaving her here.

I make Maria promise she won't leave the building until I come for her. It takes a full hour of coaxing before she agrees. There are many tears and countless declarations that I'm misguided, that I'm damned. She continues to teeter on the edge. In one moment I'm convinced she'd follow me to hell. In the next I think it wise to barricade the door.

But in the end she chooses to stay.

"I love you, Deacon," she says.

"I love you too, Maria."

She breaks down again. I hold her close until the storm passes.

"Why didn't the Teacher fight back?" she asks. "Why did he let them take him? He's so powerful. We've witnessed him do such mighty things, haven't we? Why not resist those crooked men? It would have been so simple. He could have done it without harming a hair on their heads. I don't understand."

I speak softly. "Because…he isn't the One. Once we've liberated our people, the Teacher will be of great use to our nation. But for now, for tonight, he must remain with the religious authorities. I hope you'll understand that I had to use him. He was our bargaining chip. It was the only way Henrik would have agreed. I've lined his pockets, and so have the religious authorities. They've paid a monumental price to have the Teacher silenced for the Great Festival. Don't you see? This way everyone wins. The religious authorities calm down. The Kingdom stays happy. Henrik gets rich. And I get a free shot at King Charles. And then…*revolution*."

Maria, who still looks unconvinced, says, "I pray to the one true God you're right."

I draw her closer and whisper in her ear, "I am, sweet girl. I am. You have to trust me now."

I stay with her for another hour, and then I leave to prepare for the most important day of my life.

As I creep back into the heart of the city to meet up with Henrik and Jude, I experience a calm I haven't known in many months. It's the overwhelming peace that comes from knowing you've done the right thing.

The morning comes before I'm ready. The Gratitude Ceremony is scheduled for 7:00 a.m., one hour from now.

I've spent the entire night with Henrik. But Jude is nowhere to be found.

He, like all the others, vanished during the Teacher's arrest. I saw the guards shove him aside, but after that, nothing. Henrik assured me that Jude fled the city to meet up with our army beyond the city walls, which was the plan. But first he was supposed to have met me here.

This bothers me. But there's nothing I can do about it.

I have no way to communicate with him, other than to send a message through Henrik, but Henrik and I are now attached at the hip. The Nordic centurion didn't leave my side all night, nor will he until I've killed King Charles and assumed command of the army. He's my only way in and my only way out—my solitary lifeline. For this plan to work, I need my enemy's help.

I attempted to sleep for a few hours in a discreet safe house, roughly the size of a broom closet, but it was of no use. Henrik, however, slept soundly. He probably dreamt about what he'll do with my money once he has safely fled North America and the grasp of the Kingdom he's betrayed.

A hundred times I've envisioned slitting his throat. It would be so easy. Just pull out Petra's switchblade and cut his jugular. He'd be dead within a minute. To watch him die would give me pure satisfaction. But I wouldn't do it that fast. First I'd wake him with the sharp point of the knife and ask him what he did with my parents. When he refused to answer, I'd promise to spare his life. Though he's a giant, I've already seen fear once before in his eyes. He'd tell me the truth. Once I discovered their fate, I'd ask him what it feels like to breathe but know death is moments away. Then, when his brain had processed that I was his executioner, I'd wait, perhaps for as long as ten minutes—however long it took for him to lose total control. I'd wait until he wet himself. Then, and only then, when his entire body and spirit were in the most intense anguish, I'd run the blade expertly across his neck and watch him bleed to death.

Henrik opens his eyes.

I stare at him like a lion on a lamb.

"Stop looking at me that way," he says.

"When did you decide to become a mercenary?"

"What's it to you?"

"I'm curious."

Henrik yawns and stretches his arms and legs, which run for miles. "I was orphaned as a boy. Both parents died of fever. It was just my older brother and me. It was winter, and we were starving. No vegetation grows in the Arctic that time of year. We were too dumb to hunt with any efficiency. We tried, but it was never enough. One day we were out trapping, and we saw another hunter, a lone man, in the distance. He had enough meat on his oxen to feed us for a month. We hid in the snow until he was close, and we took him."

Henrik stops talking and looks at me as though he's finished telling the story.

"It was survival," I say. "Many men would do the same in your situation and not become a hired killer."

He shakes his head. "My brother bawled for days, cried until he vomited. Even as we beat the man to death, my brother squealed, the terrible shriek of a child. Cried like a girl. The whole thing unnerved him to the core."

"But not you."

He smiles broadly. "I loved every second of it. I'd always been big and clumsy, but when the time came to kill this man, I moved like a dancer, sharp and precise. It was like a fish hatching from the egg and swimming into the sea. As the bones in his neck cracked under my hands, I thought, *So this is what the gods made me for?*" Henrik laughs. "I packed the meat the next morning and set out to find other men who might employ my newfound talent."

"And your brother?"

"I considered letting him live, chewed it over all night. But...starvation is an unkind death."

"You killed him?"

"I set him free."

"You could have learned to hunt. You killed a grown man. Animals are much easier."

Henrik stands. "I wasn't interested in hunting animals." He fastens his helmet on his head but doesn't pull down the visor. "You and I aren't that different, you know?"

"I'm nothing like you."

"You're a killer," he says. "I saw it in your eyes the night of the amphitheater fight. You were thirsty for it. A lot of men can inflict pain on a person—takes a special one to enjoy it."

I stand up. "Stop talking."

Henrik laughs softly. "You're about to kill the most powerful man on the continent, and you don't want to think of yourself as a killer? That's intriguing."

I move for the door. "Time to go."

"If you're not a killer, what are you?" he asks.

I stop, my hand on the door, and think about his question.

I think for a long while.

Then I open the door and leave, all the while begging my brain to stop sizzling.

# CHAPTER 30

Henrik's word is true. With him at my side, I proceed unchecked through the barricade. Not one member of the Centurion Guard gives me a second look after they realize we're together. They don't know me, but whoever I am, I am to be trusted.

The deception is thrilling. As we pass them, I wonder how many of these very men I'll have the privilege of slaughtering.

We climb the steps of the palace. I arrive on the landing and take my place among the other families who've been invited to the ceremony. If this were any other moment, I'd walk down the line and shake each one of their hands and express my sympathy for their losses. These are my people who have suffered a similar fate. But this isn't any other moment—it is *the moment*—and I can't afford to become emotional. I pray they survive the impending battle.

On the landing, Henrik breaks apart from me, and I slip quietly into the middle of the line, per the plan. Standing in the middle is crucial. Even with Henrik's protection and the army charging down the hill, there's still a good chance I'll be shot. I need to conceal myself among as many humans as possible to make it difficult for a sniper to get off a clean lick.

We face the palace from where King Charles will emerge, with the breathtaking view at our backs. Behind us sits a glorious city filled with God's people. I turn around for a moment and take in the scene. They're all here. The sea of people around me runs for what looks like miles. They are here for God but have come out this morning because they have no choice; King Charles must be honored. This is just one of the many ways the Kingdom desecrates our holiest holiday.

But I'm so glad they've come. They have no idea, but these Southerners are about to witness the most pivotal moment since the Kingdom overtook our land. History is about to be made. I smile warmly at my countrymen then turn back to face the Kingdom.

Trumpets announce the young king's arrival. The golden doors swing open, and King Charles appears. He's a handsome man. He has bright-green eyes that shine with intelligence and a nose that appears perfectly crafted from generations of good genes. His short-cropped hair is highlighted by natural streaks of blond from the many hours he spends outdoors. He's known as a great sportsman and a polo champion. His facial features are sharp and power-ful, and he walks like a man who owns the ground beneath his feet. He wears a red military uniform that's decorated heavily with gold medals. The heaviest cluster hangs on his right breast.

He wears no gun on his hip.

Every other man on the landing is armed to the teeth, including Henrik, who carries a black assault rifle.

King Charles is handed a microphone and he addresses the crowd. "It is with the most profound reverence that I welcome you this morning to this—*your* Holy City. And it is with supreme gratitude that I thank you for taking time from your holy festival to come meet with me, your king. On behalf of the entire Kingdom, I thank you. Your family members died in the most honorable of manner—service. While not all of them chose their destiny, they met it with dignity and grace, and for that you may be proud."

I want to ask King Charles if he was there when someone's mother died of heat exhaustion in a labor camp. I want to know whether he had the courage to look into the vacant eyes of a brother on the brink of starvation. I want to know if he personally murdered any of the people he now eulogizes. But most of all, I want to know if he's so delusional that he actually believes we care about what he's saying.

He continues, "So it is in that same spirit of pride that I honor you this morning by expressing my gratitude in an act of my own humility. You honor the deceased by your presence. I honor you with mine. May the gods of our Kingdom and your one true God bless you and your progeny forevermore."

Starting at the end of the line, King Charles bows before each person, kisses his or her hand, and rises to thank the individual face-to-face. Henrik follows closely behind, never more than a yard from the king. Henrik is the only bodyguard who moves with him. King Charles takes his time, pausing long enough to make a genuine connection with each person. The expression on his face appears sincere.

My pulse quickens. I scan the horizon. In the distance I see the outline of our army. If anyone from the Kingdom were to look, it would be obvious that men have gathered on the hill. It is a calculated risk. But if Jude were to keep the men tucked away in the surrounding woods, it would take too long to storm the city. For these last few moments, they must be exposed if we're to have any hope of succeeding.

I'm next. As the king bends down to kiss the hand of the woman next to me, I smell his musky cologne. It's an opulent odor, a tonic so fresh and clean that I wish it were on my body. I haven't had a proper bath in weeks.

The image of Maria anointing the Teacher's head with oil flashes hard and bright through my mind.

And then I meet the king.

King Charles doesn't look me in the eye before kneeling before me. He lowers his head, and I offer him my left hand. He takes it and kisses it. I pull the gun from my waistband with my other hand. I sling it around and jam the barrel beneath his chin.

No hesitation.

I pull the trigger.

The woman next to me screams.

# CHAPTER 31

The pistol bucks in my hand. The crack rings out and the king's head jerks violently backward. But his body doesn't fall limp. Time moves very slowly, but I know it's taking too long for it to happen—for him to die.

My brain has long expected chaos to follow the firing of the gun. When it doesn't come, my brain is sent into some sort of failed-expectation fog. I can't process what's happening.

The gun is still pressed beneath the king's chin. I trip the trigger again, and again it fires. But this time King Charles's hands wrap tightly around the barrel. He lifts his head slowly and lets out the most riotous laugh I've ever heard. He says, "*Oh…no.*"

He laughs uncontrollably.

"What the…?"

"Try it again," he says through a sob of laughter. "Maybe it's just jammed." He releases the gun, stands, and backs quickly away from me, still smiling and laughing. Another centurion appears instantly at his side.

I furtively glance at those standing around me. Horror and confusion blankets their faces. I look at Henrik, who says, "I think Jude warned you that gun wasn't meant to be fired." He flips the safety off his rifle and adds, "Blanks."

Before Henrik can raise his weapon, I drop the gun, pull the switchblade from my bandage, and lunge it into his thick neck.

And then chaos comes. Another screaming woman is what I hear first, before the gurgles of Henrik choking on his own blood. Then that's all I can hear, muffled choking.

I'm on the ground while a chorus of boots stomps on me. Cold steel is pressed against multiple points on my body: my head, my chest, and my groin.

Henrik twitches spastically beside me. Blood gushes from his throat like a roaring fountain; some of it lands on my lips, and I taste it. The screaming woman is eventually consumed into a larger and more cacophonic din. Madness surrounds me, but I can see nothing but the bodies and guns of the men who hold me down and pummel me.

I think I lose consciousness, but it's hard to be sure about anything right now. After an indeterminable amount of time, I'm hoisted to my feet.

King Charles greets me, looking me dead in the eye, his smile gone.

"You killed one of my men." He points to Henrik's body. A pool of dark-red blood encircles it. "Look. You did that."

I glance at Henrik. Then I notice the Southerners being honored at the Gratitude Ceremony all have been forced to their knees. A centurion stands behind each and every one.

An explosion sounds in the distance.

*The army. They should be here by now!*

I lift my eyes to scan the horizon, and a centurion strikes me hard across the face.

"Don't worry about what's happening on the hill," King Charles says. "For the moment I'd like your full attention." He dangles my gun before me. "This belonged to your father."

I spit a mouthful of blood onto his shiny black boots. "It's mine now."

"Yes, but it *was* his." He takes a beat to examine my blood on his boots. "This is the worst day of your life, Deacon. Welcome to it."

"I very much doubt that."

Another explosion shakes the ground. The thousands gathered stampede away from the palace. The earth hums from the explosion and the mass exodus.

"I heard you got off a shot the night you met your rebel army. I was worried you'd discover the blanks. But Henrik—may he rest in peace—assured me you were far too obsessed with revenge to notice something so subtle. I guess he was right."

Another explosion—this one is louder and much more violent than the first two.

It feels like we're standing on a boat; the ground rolls beneath us.

Finally it all comes together.

I say, "I was set up?"

"From the very beginning," King Charles replies.

"What's happening on the hill? Let me see my men."

King Charles raises a finger. "One moment please. I need to speak with you first. Your father was the best organizer of men the South has seen in quite some time. He did, in a few short years, what no one was capable of doing for decades. From our perspective, something had to be done about it."

"That's why my parents were arrested? You knew about their involvement in the resistance?"

"Of course we knew. I thought your father's arrest would be the end of it. Kill morale and all that. Get him to the North, torture your mother in front of him, and then he'd talk—tell us everything we didn't already know."

"You tortured my mother?"

"Yes, personally in fact."

I lunge at him, but my body feels like it's in a body cast; so many hands are on me. I struggle with every ounce of strength until another fist strikes my jaw.

"But your father didn't talk," King Charles continues, "not even as we violated your mother. He was an impenetrable vault. You should be proud of that. You also should know he and your mother suffered more than anyone in the history of my reign, and that's saying something."

I fall limp. The thought of my parents dying a cruel death is too much for me to handle. I fervently had prayed they'd met a quick fate. Discovering that they suffered greatly *is* the worst moment of my life.

"I'm not sure you have any pertinent information for me, but we'll see. For the moment it's enough that you brought your money and your army to us."

"What's happening with my men?"

"Aren't you worried about the money?"

"Show me the hill," I say.

King Charles gives the nod of approval, and his guards usher me across the landing until I have a clear view of the hill. A large plume of smoke rises high in the air.

I know the truth before he tells me.

They're all dead.

The king proudly gazes at the ridge. "My soldiers didn't attack until your men could see that I rose from the dead, that your gunshot couldn't kill me," he says. "A few men were allowed to retreat alive so they may return home and spread word of this defeat, your death, and the desecration of their army. The rest were butchered."

I have no words. The men…they're all…I can't believe it. I fall to my knees, and the centurions let me.

"As with your father, you should be proud, Deacon. This is the first time in ages I've actually been concerned about an uprising. Those men were committed to your father; they believed in you." He smiles and slaps me on the back. "Thank the gods you came home."

The centurions lift me to my feet.

King Charles continues, "Someone here needs to pay for Henrik's bloodshed. Since you're having such a bad day, Deacon, I'll give you the honor of choosing the sacrifice. Which one of these people…" He gestures to the families on the landing. "…should have the honor of dying for your sins?"

"You want me to…*choose?*"

"Yes, and quickly, if it's not too much trouble."

"I…*no.* None of them should die."

"Very well then. All shall. Centurion Guard! Raise your rifles!"

Each centurion positioned behind the families trains his weapon on the back of a Southern head.

"No!" I shout. "Kill me! I deserve to die. Shoot me instead!"

King Charles looks disappointed. He shakes his head like a teacher fed up with a derelict student. "No, Deacon, you can't die yet. Now choose. I won't ask again."

The people on their knees quake with fear. They look to me in utter despair, their eyes wide.

I plead with the king. "I can't. "Please…you've already massacred my army. Spill no more blood. It's the Great Festival!"

"Says the man who just put a gun beneath my chin and pulled the trigger!"

"*Please!*" I beg him.

King Charles gives the signal, and the shots are fired.

171

# CHAPTER 32

I 'm taken beneath the palace and thrown into a dingy holding cell. My arms and legs are shackled. I've never been in such agony. My head aches and my ribs feel shattered. Every breath is like a dagger in my side.

The physical pain, however, is nothing compared to my emotional trauma. I'm a total failure. My men are dead. All those families are dead. The resistance has been thwarted.

And Maria is alone.

I'm sobbing uncontrollably on the cold stone floor when his voice rolls forth from a dark corner of my cell. "Why do you weep, my friend?"

It's the Teacher.

He hobbles forward on his knees and collapses next to me. He's bleeding and in terrible pain. He moans with every breath.

"What have they done to you?" I say.

"The religious authorities handed me over to King Charles."

"I...I'm sorry," I tell him.

Our cell door opens, and King Charles himself glides in. A cadre of centurions accompanies him. I brace myself for more pain, but they're not here for me. The men grab hold of the Teacher and lift him to his feet. They leave me where I lie.

King Charles examines the Teacher, looking him up and down as if purchasing a slave. "Your own religious authorities say you've broken many laws."

The Teacher doesn't answer. Instead he looks down at me with his kind eyes. He must know I was complicit in his betrayal, but still he looks to me as a friend, as a brother.

King Charles says, "Are you this so-called king of the South, as your followers say? The messiah come to set them free...or whatever?"

"If you say so," the Teacher replies.

"They've charged you with serious crimes. Have you no answer?"

The Teacher says nothing more. From what I've heard, King Charles has never, in his life, had a man refuse to answer his questions. I can see this astounds him. This almighty man, who has just executed innocent families, is shaken—as we all are—by the presence of the Teacher.

"Very well," the king tells the centurions. "Bring them both up to the landing. The people are clamoring for the customary release of a prisoner. I never should have instituted this tradition, but I feel this year it may actually be put to good use. We'll let them choose which one of you two they want back—the miracle worker or the bumbling rebel with the blood of his own people on his hands." King Charles kicks me in the ribs and I roar in pain. "Who do you think they'll choose, Deacon?"

I don't say a word as the Teacher and I are led outside, where there aren't nearly as many people as before. But several thousand are still crowded in front of the palace landing. The Teacher and I, in chains, are both presented to the people.

Chaos ensues in the Holy City. The ridge where my men lie dead is still smoking, and the blood from those killed on the landing hasn't yet been mopped up. In the crowd small riots are erupting, no doubt in response to the mass execution.

Everywhere I turn I see centurions beating people. I watch as a woman is ripped from her clothing and dragged out of sight. Her child screams in horror; no one comes to rescue him.

King Charles addresses the people. "Every year at the Great Festival, I give back to you one of your own. Given the terrible but necessary bloodshed of today, I feel this ritual holds special significance. We must work together in partnership if we're ever to hope for everlasting peace. Now shall I release to you the Teacher, the so-called king of the South? This man who preaches a message of peace, hope, and love? Is this who you'd like freed from his chains?"

The people shout a reply, but it's impossible to decipher any sort of consensus. King Charles, who clearly has no intention of letting me go, asks the question again. "Whom shall I return to you? This man who has committed no crime? Or this murderer, rebel, and attempted assassin? The man who tried to steal *my* very life?"

I spot Fat Belly and Gray Beard perched at the front of the crowd. They orchestrate the chant. It rises fast from the people and slams into our ears with gale force. "Deacon! Deacon! Deacon! Deacon! Deacon!"

King Charles's face goes white; his chin trembles with shock and anger. He confers privately with his men, who are undoubtedly advising him to listen to the crowd. The people already have been pushed to their limits. One more insult, and they're likely to revolt—all of them.

But why do they chant my name? I've failed them. I'm not their messiah, and the Teacher has done nothing wrong. Fat Belly and Gray Beard catch my eye; they're manipulating the crowd for their own purposes. They despise the Teacher because he challenges their authority, their power, their way of life. They'll stop at nothing to see him discredited, to see him condemned.

The mob cries out for my release.

King Charles turns back to the crowd. "But why? What evil has the Teacher done? What crime has he committed?"

They only cry louder, "Deacon! Deacon! Deacon! Deacon! Deacon!"

King Charles looks like he is ready to explode, but he reigns in his emotion. "Then what do you wish me to do with the man you call the 'king of the South'?"

Fat Belly says it first. It doesn't take long for the others to concur. Gray Beard raises his fists. Fat Belly cups his hands over his mouth and hollers. Soon the verdict is unanimous.

They shout, "Crucify him!"

King Charles reluctantly nods and the centurions throw me off the landing and into the crowd.

People trample me as they storm away to the palace courtyard where the Teacher will be flogged before his execution. I try to get up, but the herd of people knocks me back to the ground.

I decide to die and am amazed by how quickly I accept it.

I've caused irrevocable damage. I've been played for a fool. I've caused my people—those I was supposed to liberate—more death and sorrow. I'm not just a failure; I'm a murderer. King Charles is right; their blood is on my hands.

Someone stomps my chest, but I no longer feel any pain because my mind is floating back in time. Back to Jude.

Why didn't I see it? How could I have been so naïve?

He played me from the start. It must have always been a double cross. He worked both sides. Who knows how far back it goes, but at some point the Kingdom got to him. They knew he was close with my father, and they turned him. Jude betrayed the South to get rich. All they needed was to get me home.

Take away my parents. Show me the money. Give me the gun. Lead me to the men. Shut down the resistance; snuff out the rebellion.

It was so simple—so tragically simple—yet I danced to their music like a drunken fool.

Jude gave the Kingdom my army, and he got me to help deliver the Teacher to the religious authorities. It was a win-win for everyone eager to see life continue as is.

Especially for Jude, who stole all my money.

Dr. Stone and Henrik never betrayed their Kingdom.

I bite my tongue, as if chewing through a tough piece of meat, and try to sever it. I beg my heart to stop pumping. I hold my breath.

The pain rises inside me like lava to the brim of a volcano. The pressure in my head nears detonation.

I'm alive.

Still alive.

Still alive.

Then I fade. I can't breathe. The pain is unreal. I'm past the tipping point. I slide away. Here it comes…death.

*Take me, please!*

Wet lips snatch my spirit as it rises slowly from my body. Small hands push it back down into my chest. A tender voice relaxes my jaw and opens my eyes.

Maria.

It is always Maria. She says, "Come, before it's too late."

I breathe in and choke on the air. I begin to speak, but she presses a finger to my lips and helps me to my feet.

The pain is intolerable. I drape my arm around her and hobble as she leads me through the rough sea of people. We follow the others until we're led to where the Teacher has been taken.

The flogging already has begun. The Kingdom has stripped the Teacher naked and chained him to a post. He's on his knees. A centurion cracks a whip against his back, and he writhes in pain. Maria shouts for them to stop; others plead for mercy.

But others—many others—cheer their approval.

In shock, I say nothing. I think of how it should be me, and not him, taking this beating.

A centurion flogs the Teacher until there is no longer skin on his back; it's a muddy river of blood and exposed muscles and tendons. I can see the white of bone. He bleeds so profusely that I think he'll die at any moment. No man can survive such punishment, such unfettered violence.

When the flogging is finished, the Teacher is lifted to his feet and clothed in a purple cloak. One of the centurions shoves a crown of thorns onto his head. Blood drips off his eyebrows. They salute him, saying, "Hail the Teacher, the king of the South!" Each centurion takes a turn bowing in sarcastic respect before him. Rising up, they spit in his face and strike his head repeatedly, until his eyes, which never have done anything but emit kindness, fill with blood.

When they're satisfied, they strip him once again and put his pants back on him. Then they lead him out of the courtyard to crucify him.

The Teacher is in no condition to carry his own cross.

The centurions compel a man who is passing by to carry it for him. They point a gun in his face and order him to do it. He complies.

Our dark procession leads us out of the city and up a hill known locally as "the Skull." Atop the hill the centurions lay his cross on the ground and prepare to nail the Teacher to it.

Maria helps me along until we get as close to the Teacher as possible, which is about the dumbest thing she and I could do. If I were smart, I'd take Maria away from this place, and I'd do it now, at this very moment.

Everything is lost, destroyed. I was completely wrong, and Maria knew it all along. Yet here we are, both alive and together. We can still escape and find our life together. We can still go to Mexico. I want that so terribly.

I search the small crowd that has come to the Skull to witness this death on a cross.

There is no Miles. No Petra. No Jude. I don't see a single person from our group; not one of the Teacher's students is here. Maria is the one who has stuck by his side, the only one unafraid to be associated with him.

"Why did you leave the safe house?" I ask her. "You could have been killed."

"Petra came to me," she says. "He found Jude last night, moments before he—"

"*What?* Petra saw Jude? Where is he?"

"Dead," she says. "He hanged himself. He confessed his sins to Petra. Then he told him where I was."

"I can't believe he's dead. He has my money. He can't be dead."

"The Teacher's prophecy about Petra was true—about the denial. Before the cock crowed, Petra denied knowing the Teacher three separate times. Can you believe that? He was distraught, rambling like a madman. I tried to calm him, but it was of no use. I don't have a clue where he is now."

Picturing Jude hanging and Petra as a madman spins my head. "How did you know I was in trouble?"

"I didn't leave the safe house for you," she says," her eyes fixed on the Teacher, who's being offered a final cup of wine mixed with myrrh. "I came for him. I came for my beloved messiah."

"I understand," I say softly. Tears stream down my face as I watch centurions lift nails and hammers.

The Teacher is affixed to the cross. It is nine in the morning and brutally hot. The centurions drive nails through his hands and feet. He screams wildly. Above his head an inscription reads, THE KING OF THE SOUTH.

Two other men are crucified with him. Both are bandits, we're told, one on his right and one on his left.

We watch the Teacher die. It takes a very long time.

During his torture many people pass by and mock him, saying, "Aha! You who would destroy the temple and build it in three days, save yourself, come down from the cross."

I pray to the one true God that he will. Even now—now that I understand his path is the truer path to freedom—I don't understand why he doesn't save himself from this death. Why not pull the nails from his body and heal his own wounds?

Fat Belly and Gray Beard appear along with a cohort of religious leaders and other holy men. Gray Beard says, "He saved others, yet he can't save himself."

Fat Belly adds, "Let the messiah, the king of the South, come down from the cross now, so that we may see and believe."

Even the dying men to the Teacher's right and left taunt him.

At noon the clouds roll in. For the next three hours, the sky is as dark as night. Thunder booms overhead, but no rain comes. The earth is angry.

At three in the afternoon, the Teacher lifts his weary head to the heavens. "My God, my God," he says, "why have you forsaken me?"

Maria and I hold each other close.

I say, "Death has drawn near to him."

"He's quoting the Scripture," Maria says. Then from memory, she recites, "'My God, my God, why have you forsaken me? And are so far from my cry and from the words of my distress?'"

"I remember pieces of it," I say. "'Many young bulls encircle me; strong bulls of Bashan surround me. They open wide their jaws at me, like a ravening lion. I am poured out like water; all my bones are out of joint; my heart within my breast is melting wax.' That's all I can remember."

Maria nuzzles her head into my chest and whispers, "'For kingship belongs to the Lord; he rules over the nations. To him alone all who sleep in the earth bow down in worship; all who go down to the dust fall before him.'"

"Yes," I say. I remember it now. "'My soul shall live for him; my descendants shall serve him; they shall be known as the Lord's forever.'"

We speak the final line together. "'They shall come and make known to a people yet unborn the saving deeds that he has done.'"

One of the centurions, a short man with dark skin, fills a sponge with sour wine, puts it on a stick, and raises it to the Teacher's mouth. Another centurion says, "Wait, let's see whether his prophets will come to take him down."

*Yes*, I think. *Save him!* I pray to the one true God and plead on the Teacher's behalf. If he is your messiah, bring him down from the cross and lift him up. Give him the power to overthrow this wicked Kingdom.

178

But nothing happens. The heavens do not open. The God of our ancestors does not intervene. There will be no last-second clemency for the Teacher.

Instead he gives a loud cry and breathes his last.

The earth shakes violently beneath us. The quake is so fierce that many onlookers are knocked off their feet. A look of uncertainty creeps across the callous-faced centurions. Maria sobs into my chest. "Is he really dead?" she says. "Can it be true?"

"He's gone," I say flatly, stunned by the quake. "He no longer suffers."

When the earthquake finishes its rumble, the centurion standing closest to the cross turns toward us and, with amazement in his voice, says, "Truly this man was God's son!"

His words cut me in half. Could this be right? Did the one true God send the Teacher? I stare up at his lifeless face and am haunted by my own thoughts: A messiah is either victorious or he dies.

Maria runs toward the cross. I chase after her. "Maria! Wait. We must leave! Now!"

She falls to her knees and reaches for his bloodied feet. His body doesn't move.

I fall to my knees next to her as the sky finally releases its water. Everything inside me tells me to run, to take Maria and escape. My survival instincts roar within me. *Get out! Do it now! While you still can!*

But I don't rise.

Instead I sob for my sin.

I sob for my betrayal.

I sob for my parents.

I sob for my dead army.

I sob for my fellow Southerners.

I sob for the innocent man I condemned.

I sob for Maria, for not being the man she needs.

I sob for fear that I have just killed God's son.

Then it gets worse.

I'm yanked from the mud by my shoulders. Shackles are quickly secured around my hands and legs. Another is fastened around my neck. A fresh-faced centurion, one who has just arrived at the scene, says, "King Charles heard that you were here, that you hadn't fled the city."

"No!" Maria screams.

"Shut up!" the centurion yells at her. He refocuses his murderous stare on me. With a smile he says, "The venerable King Charles wishes to see you."

# CHAPTER 33

My meeting with King Charles was brief. All he said was, "You and I will speak in the North, after we've fled this Southern hell. If you behave yourself, I might let you speak to your mother."

"What!"

But the king just waved his hand in dismissal. "Take him away!"

That was three days ago. My departure date has arrived.

We board the train like cattle to the slaughter. We prisoners are herded en masse and without regard for individual dignity, for we have ceased to be human in the eyes of the Kingdom. All that matters now is that the group is shoved aboard and the train departs on time.

The centurions don't show an ounce of concern for those among us who are so obviously ill that a long journey is the equivalent of a death sentence. It simply doesn't matter that a significant number of us won't be alive when we arrive at the station in the North.

I'm shirtless, and shackles are latched around my wrists and ankles. The centurions prod us along with stun guns, shocking anyone who dares stumble or hesitate for even a fraction of a second. I've already been shocked once for a look of defiance, but I made a vow, and even now I won't bow my eyes to these men—the men who killed my Lord and stole my love from me.

Most of the prisoners accept their fate stoically. But as we climb the ladder into the train, we hear cries from a woman in the next car over. She's wailing for her family, telling the guards her husband is ill and unable to care for their children. Taking her north will doom her entire family. I'm glad the same can't be said for Maria, who wasn't arrested. She'll survive with or without me; her spirit is untiring. But I worry about Alejandro. He's out there, looming, and Maria is alone.

I'm badly injured and deeply depressed. I don't know if I believe King Charles, but if there's even the slightest chance my mother is alive, I must survive this train ride. This hope keeps me going.

A centurion warns the sobbing woman to shut her mouth. The woman, however, doesn't heed the warning. The centurion warns her again and finally a third time. When the poor soul doesn't comply, we hear the sharp crack of a pistol, a sickening groan, and a deafening silence.

The gunshot halts our progress, and we wait to hear what will happen next, but nothing does. The guards behind us bellow for us to keep moving, and we collectively realize they have no intention of removing the dead body from the train. The men in that car will make the journey with a bloody, rotting carcass in tow. It's nearly one hundred degrees outside; the stench will be unbearable by noon.

I shuffle into the car and make my way to the rear, where I'm jammed against a small open window. Luckily it's wide enough for me to stick my head through and gulp a mouthful of fresh air. It's a small but magnificent stroke of good fortune, and I thank God for his small mercies.

The guards pack our car tightly, shoulder to shoulder; there must be fifty people per car. We sit balled up on the bloodstained floor, our knees pulled high to our chins, doing our best to pretend we don't know what's already taken place on this train—that countless souls have been dragged away from life to death.

Panic erupts in my brain, fast and searing. There's no room to move or to stretch. We're trapped. My eyes flash wildly at the people around me. The truth hits me. We're not in a train car—we're in a coffin.

One man already has defecated on the floor near me. The fresh air from the window does nothing to mask the smell of human waste. The journey north will take at least twenty-four hours, and I suspect this car will arrive in hell long before we reach the North.

Moments later the car door clangs shut, and the train slowly moves forward. And there it is; none of us will ever return home. We will never again lay eyes on the beautiful countryside of our ancestors, the land stolen from us before we were even born.

As the train gathers speed, I hear my name called faintly in the distance. I turn toward the window, but no one is there. The train chugs on…faster and faster. The conductor pulls the whistle, and the steel beast screams the shrill cry of departure.

I hear my name again. This time the voice is louder and more urgent.

I jerk my head out the window, and there I see her, running in the light of the rising sun.

Maria has lifted her dress just above her knees, and she runs recklessly toward the train. I struggle to move, to try to peel myself out of the doomed car, but I barely can move an inch. I crane my neck and perilously poke my head out the window. It's an excruciatingly awkward angle, like that of a baby born with its face pointing upward.

"Maria!" I cry out. "Here! Maria! It's Deacon!"

The woman I love sees me and manages to narrowly slip past a centurion who lunges for her. I see another raise his rifle and aim it directly at her chest. "No!" I scream. "No!"

She cries out to me, running alongside our train, just as my mother did a lifetime ago. "Deacon! Deacon!" she hollers.

"Yes! Maria! I'm right here!"

She yells something, but the screaming whistle and the chug of engines drown out her voice.

"What?" I say. "What is it?"

She calls out again, but it's useless; I can't hear her. All I can think to do is say the only thing that still matters. "Maria! I love you!" I choke on my words, swallow hard, and yell again, "I love you!"

"The Teacher!" she gasps, as the whistle finishes its scream. Maria reaches the end of the platform and stops hard to avoid tumbling off the edge and onto the tracks. The centurion fires, and Maria's chest splits open. Falling, she cries out, "He has risen!"

# AUTHOR BIO

Ryan Casey Waller was born and raised in Texas, and educated at the University of Southern California, Perkins School of Theology at SMU, and Dedman School of Law at SMU. You can find him at www.ryancaseywaller. com or somewhere in the great city of Dallas.

Made in the USA
Charleston, SC
28 February 2014